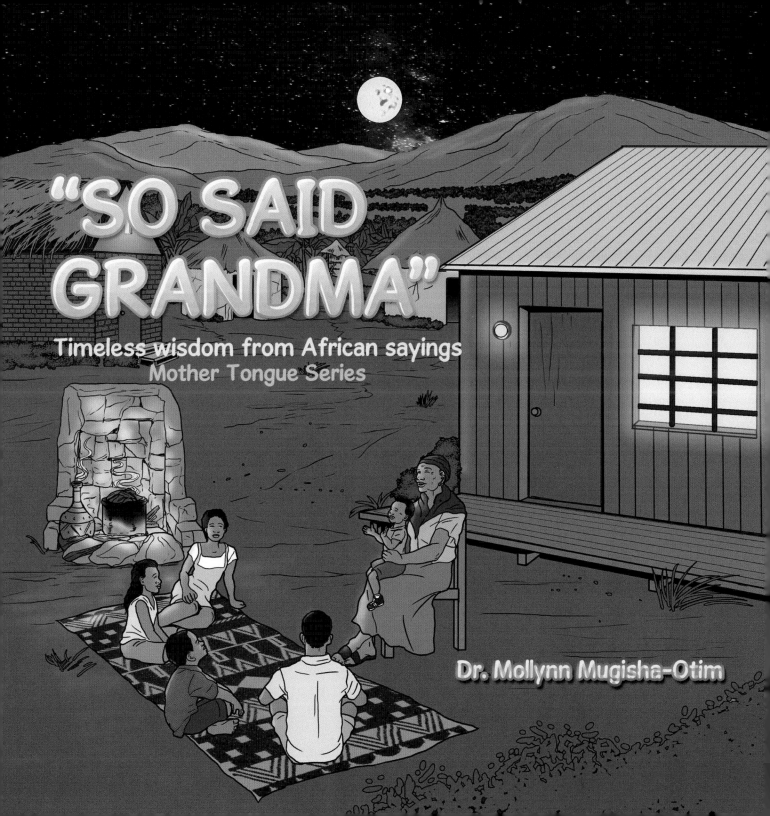

AuthorHouse™ UK
1663 Liberty Drive
Bloomington, IN 47403 USA
www.authorhouse.co.uk
Phone: 0800 047 8203 (Domestic TFN)
+44 1908 723714 (International)

Because of the dynamic nature of the Internet, any web addresses or links contained in this book may have changed
since publication and may no longer be valid. The views expressed in this work are solely those of the author and do
not necessarily reflect the views of the publisher, and the publisher hereby disclaims any responsibility for them.

Any people depicted in stock imagery provided by Getty Images are models,
and such images are being used for illustrative purposes only.
Certain stock imagery © Getty Images.

This book is printed on acid-free paper.

Author photo by Fotografie Americaine

ISBN: 978-1-7283-9030-7 (sc)
ISBN: 978-1-7283-9031-4 (e)

Print information available on the last page.

Published by AuthorHouse 03/31/2020

authorHOUSE®

CONTENTS

DEDICATION

This book is dedicated to my loving grandmother Mrs. Elvania Kashesya (kaaka). The memory of your love, patience and generosity inspires me each day. You will continue to live in our hearts, and through the works of this book.

EPIGRAPH

A very interesting read. Some sayings were not hard to understand because of the existence of similar ones in Dutch. But some were surprising. Mollynn has written a book that gives you a fun way to learn more about the day-to-day Ugandan life and culture. I really enjoyed translating the sayings into Dutch.

Marjolein Meinderts-Weber (Translate-M)

PREFACE AND ACKNOWLEDGEMENTS.

As a mother born and raised in Uganda, but raising my own children in Europe, I often found myself struggling to teach and explain certain concepts to them. These were concepts embodying values that were central to living happily as individuals yet recognizing that they are also part of a community. I felt that these were passed on easily from generation to generation as proverbs and wise sayings in the setting of African communal societies. Because these wise sayings are not written down in fun and educative books for the young children to read, they are likely to soon be forgotten. This realization, coupled with the desire to ensure that our young multicultural generation does not miss out on this wealth of wisdom from African sayings, I decided to write this book, "SO SAID GRANDMA, *wisdom from African sayings*" for my children and others like them growing up among cultures.

Special thanks to my brother, Arnold Ainamani, who helped me with remembering and filling in the memory gaps for some of the stories of our childhood that I had almost forgotten. Also special thanks to my children who accepted to listen to the drafts of the book in place of their usual bedtime stories, and provided valuable feedback that made me realise that I needed to simplify the stories and language for the young readers.

FOREWORD

I met Mollynn in 2007. She had applied to work with me at my childcare company in The Netherlands. She never made it to the interview though! She got lost in this new country that she had arrived to recently. Her husband had been relocated to work in The Netherlands and she came along with him. I waited for her to arrive and messaged back and forth for directions. Eventually I decided to take my car and drive to meet her at a public swimming pool where she found herself at!

I will never forget that moment. I walked in to meet this lovely bright happy joyful face looking up with a smile. From that moment on Mollynn was the heart and soul of my company. Every parent and child at Zein Childcare adored her. She worked in every department and she glided with ease from branch to branch as a teacher or a nurse, as a manager and an educator. She even worked in our ever-growing business support office and Human Resource Department when the need arose.

Mollynn is one of the kindest and most loving people I ever met. She is an example of strength, faith, stability and she carries joy with her everywhere she goes. When life or work are stressful; Mollynn doesn't stress. When big growth blessed our business bringing endless tasks and unenforceable changes, she didn't fuss. She simply faced every challenge with a smile and joy. She made difficulties seem like a 'normal' part of life! Which they are! She showed people around her how to accept challenges and learn from them. She is a well of knowledge and deep strength. As Mollynn worked in many departments at Zein Childcare; it didn't matter to her if the role moved her up or down! She knew who she was and she knew her worth. She simply had faith that it was for the higher good for everyone involved. She was an island of solitude in an ocean of changes. An example for others and a peaceful presence.

I am proud to be her friend and honored to write this fore ward. It is with joy and excitement that I introduce this book to you. I know that everything Mollynn does, comes from the heart and is blessed with joy aiming to benefit others. I am so happy to see her work finally in a book print that will reach people worldwide and make them smile, laugh, learn and enjoy.

Mollynn is a beautiful soul who is a blessing to everyone around her. She is a JOY.

Robbie Zein

Robbie Zein - is an expatriate educational consultant specialised in childcare for the international community. She is the founder of Zein child care Group; the largest international childcare provider in Europe. She is the author of the book "CHOICES" which offers parents and educators a calm and punishment-free guidance system for children. She currently lectures for international schools and organisations worldwide.

INTRODUCTION:

I was born in a small village in the South Western Uganda called Kati. Kati is in present day Mitooma district, Ruhinda subcounty. I spent the first 8 years of my life with my grandmother whom we all called "Kaaka". Growing up with her was a memorable experience. The life lessons I learned from her and other elders have shaped who I am today. She taught and guided us all with love, patience and understanding. Most of all, I remember that with her, there was no need for many words because she always spoke in wise sayings. These sayings were not exclusive to her, they were a way of life, known, used and understood by everyone. People used them naturally. One saying could explain a whole lesson that no amount of words could make clearer. These sayings were a memorable way to impart wisdom from one generation to the next. It did not matter if one went to school or not because these were part of the oral traditional method of education. They were not written down in books, they were taught as stories.

I have felt the urge to share some of my favorite and most memorable sayings for a while. I believe that this legacy of language and culture is the best gift I can share with my children, and all those growing up around the world, who may not have the privilege I had to hear it in grandmother's own words.

In this book, I will share 41 of my favorite sayings in 9 chapters. Each chapter has a category of sayings with a common moral lesson. Each saying is meant to teach certain lessons ranging from love, patience, unity, discipline, courage, kindness, responsibility, focus and expected social behaviour.

The sayings are written in Runyankore-Rukiga, a language also known as Runyakitara. They are then translated to English and Dutch. Effort has been made to make these translations as direct as possible without losing the meaning, while ensuring that the translation still makes sense in the contemporary world. Therefore, some meanings may not be immediately obvious until one reads more into the explanation. In cases where a close equivalent saying in Dutch or other language is known, it is stated.

I present a blending together of ancient folklore with experiences in modern day to day examples. There is also a mix of myth and reality in some of the stories. This creates interesting scenarios. I also share some interesting stories and experiences that help make the lessons clearer. I hope you enjoy reading it as much as I enjoyed writing it.

A lady puzzled by the long "to-do-list" on her day off.

CHAPTER 1:

PATIENCE.

This chapter is a collection of 4 of my favourite sayings that taught me to work hard with patience. I learned that small actions performed well can have great results. I also learned to always think of possible consequences of my actions.

Amaisho n'amooro.

Eyes are lazy.
Ogen zijn lui
(Nederlandse uitdrukking: ogen misleiden)

Eyes help us see what is right in front of us. Because the eyes do not perform any actions, we can only make assumptions and estimations of what needs to be done by seeing. This saying explains why just seeing with eyes can be misleading and bring about laziness or discouragement. Humans have the power to foresee,make predictions and plan ahead of time. This planning is not done with the eyes.

However, most people tend to be discouraged by the size and scope of their tasks, ambitions and goals. Eyes do not see with values like patience and consistency of effort. So, it can be discouraging when it looks like there is too much to do and too little time. You feel lazy because you cannot see where to start. But once you take the first step and start, you get so immersed in the task that you accomplish a lot in no time.

Looking at an example of the days we used to cultivate land with a hand hoe. Early morning when you reached on the piece of land to dig, it initially looked too big to be finished in one day. But when we started with one dig at a time, in a few hours it was done. Sometimes we were surprised by how big the land we had managed to dig at the end of the day was.

Whenever you look at a task that seems so big, remember that "looking with eyes only can be deceptive". Just get started and you can indeed surprise yourself in the end by how much you have done, and how fast you have done it. Always remember that "eyes are lazy". Practice seeing beyond what physical eyes can see. This practice helps improve your imagination but also your patience to do something a step at a time

Kamwe kamwe nigwe omuganda

One by one makes a bundle
Een voor een maakt een bundel / Strootje voor strootje maak je een bezem

This saying was commonly used by my grandmother. She used it to teach me how every little bit of help matters.

A common example that helped me understand this better was using a broom made of straw. Although the broom is the whole bundle, it is actually made of single strands of straw. To make the whole bundle, you need every single strand. so, 1 by 1 collected together, makes the bundle.

A hand broom commonly used to sweep and clean the floor

An example is if you were thinking of accomplishing a big task. You would need to look at it as the bundle. However, that big task is made up of many small individual actions. These actions put together would make the complete task.

For example, imagine if you need to save money for something. Something so big that you need a lot of money. In order to save a lot of money you need to save small amounts consistently over a period of time. Consider, for example, €1.00 saved every day or every week. Eventually you would save the money you need. Yet the €1.00 individually looks small compared to the total amount. So when you look at getting the big money it might appear like a very hard task, but when you look at saving little by little it is possible that you have the big amount eventually.

The same can apply to any aspect of life. For example, behaviour. If someone does something bad (that is not allowed) once, she may think of it as something small that really doesn't matter. This could be any bad behaviour like lying; stealing; refusing to eat certain foods for no reason; being mean to a sibling or being late for an activity, etc. If this is done occasionally, it may be seen as one small undesirable act that doesn't really matter. But in the end many undesirable acts repeated over time soon become bad habits and these habits make undesirable behaviour. This can result in someone being known as a badly-behaved person. Small bad acts repeated can make a big bad situation. This is because they accumulate over time. Someone who quarrels many times becomes a quarrelsome person, someone who fights a lot becomes a violent person, someone who dodges chores a lot becomes a lazy person.

It also works in a positive way. If you want to learn something good or become good at something like maths or sports or good behaviour, you just need to do something small about it every day. Look at it like practicing. At the start, it may not feel so easy. As you persist and do it often, you become better each day. Practice makes for improvement.

It is also similar to the saying that *"Every journey of a thousand miles begins with a single step."* You have to take a step and many more to finish the journey. But it is one step at a time to complete the journey.

However big or hard a goal may seem, always go for it and work patiently, you will make a real joyful bundle of success before you know it. Always remember that *"kamwe kamwe nigwe omuganda,"* One by one makes a bundle.

Ekiro kimwe tikikajunzya enyama.

Leaving meat to stay one night cannot make it go bad/rot.

Als je vlees slechts één nacht bewaart, kan het niet bederven (Nederlandse uitdrukking: Wat in het vat zit, verzuurt niet)

Meat is one of the most perishable foods. Once it's not preserved well, it will go bad in a short time. When it goes bad, it stinks and you cannot eat it, otherwise you get really sick. Because meat is expensive, it is extremely important that it is cooked immediately, or preserved well to stay good longer. In those days there was no electricity or fridges to store meat to keep it fresh. The only way to preserve it was to salt it (by putting a lot of salt and drying it) or to roast it with smoke till it was dry. So the proverb says that "if you let the meat stay overnight for only one day, it will not go bad". It was a way to teach that some things can wait one day and are not as urgent as they may seem at first. Therefore, our elders wanted us to know that sometimes when something is not done overnight, it doesn't mean that is a disaster.

This taught us to be patient in some situations especially if the conditions at hand were not favorable. As children, we needed to be a little patient, even for a day. Sometimes one needed to wait for a week, or a month or even longer. We also learned as young children, that having some things in life or not getting them when we wanted, is not the end of the world.

As a child, I loved playdates and sometimes sleepovers at cousins' homes. I remember one day, I had a play date planned for Saturday. But my parents got so busy that it was postponed. I don't remember exactly what urgent thing my parents had to do. I think my little sister was also sick. The sleep-over was postponed to the following weekend. I cried and lamented about how unfair it was, but my mother kept telling me "*ekiro kiimwe tikizunzya enyama*". You can imagine I was too upset to care. Waiting another week seemed like the end of the world. In the end I calmed down, but can you imagine I survived the week? Of course I did! Because leaving meat to stay one night cannot make it go bad. Gradually I learned to be patient when things didn't go as I wanted. I still find the value of patience useful even as an adult.

<u>Food for thought</u>

Can you remember some times in your life when it has been a challenge to be patient?

Otariho tagweerwa omuti.

A person who is not present cannot be hit by a falling tree"
Iemand die er niet is, kan niet geraakt worden door een omvallende boom

If a tree falls and you are not right under it, you cannot be hit by it. Imagine a person cutting a tree, it can only fall on people who are standing around it. Anyone who is not around at that moment will not be affected or hit by the tree.

This saying was to teach us that an immediate situation cannot affect someone who is not involved in it. This proverb was used often by our parents as we grew up. In cases when something was to be shared among family members and a few threatened to go away or refused to eat because they were upset, my mother would use this saying. This would automatically remind you that if you are not there, your share will not be kept. She didn't want to encourage the habit that when you are upset, you refuse to eat. This was also good to prevent unnecessary movements from home to go roaming around the village at mealtimes. Knowing this, we made sure that we were home for meals. In the long run, patience was taught to young people as a vital aspect of value in life.

I remember one time I went to a birthday party of a classmate. While I was away, an auntie visited and brought sweet treats to share. All were eaten and when I came back, I heard about it and run to mummy for my treat. She casually told me *"otariho tagwerwa omuti!"* I was so disappointed that I cried. I kept telling her that "it's not fair!". Then she reminded me that while I enjoyed the party, my siblings were bored at home. So, there is no unfairness that they had a treat. I learned that we all don't get the same advantages and that doesn't mean it's unfair. Sometimes there is an element of luck but also being in the right place at the right time

The Baganda in central Uganda have a saying that: "*Omumpi wakooma wakwaata*"- It means that a short person can only touch where they can reach. A short person cannot touch what they cannot reach. People have different talents and abilities (consider height in this case). Some people may be able to do certain things or have certain abilities, while others may not. Each one should appreciate what they have. For example, someone may seem to have better toys than others. Don't feel bad because there are some other things you may have more of, that they don't have at all.

Can you imagine how boring life would be if we all looked alike, had the same things, the same qualities and liked the same things? It is commonly said that "*variety is the spice of life*" Don't feel bad when something good happens to someone else and not you. Just imagine that the tree of that good thing fell when you were away. You will be hit by another tree so just be patient and keep living your life happily.

*Grandma telling stories to the children
in the courtyard after dinner*

CHAPTER 2:

DISCIPLINE

In this chapter, I share some favourite sayings that taught me how to behave well, pay attention to advice and learn self-control.

Ningambira abaheiguru, ngu na abahansi bahurire.

When I am talking to the people on a higher level, I expect the ones on the lower level to be listening too.

Als ik spreek tegen mensen op een hoger niveau, verwacht ik dat degenen op het lagere niveau ook luisteren.

People on a higher level usually meant older children while lower level meant younger ones. While our parents rebuked one of us after doing something wrong, they directed words to the whole family. This meant that if someone was in the wrong and was being punished, it was a chance for the rest to learn not to repeat the same mistake. This was to avoid repeating the same advice time after time on the same issue. It also meant that one could not say "I didn't know," yet they were present when someone else was corrected for the same action. It was expected for everyone around, young or old to learn from your fellow siblings' mistakes. Being an older sibling came with the responsibility of being an example in modeling good behaviour for younger ones. Older children were usually punished first and more severely for the same mistake because they were expected to know better. It was also so that the young ones could watch and learn. Thus, this proverb was developed from this act of punishing the older one (who are on a higher level) for the young ones (who are on a lower level) to learn and avoid the mistakes in future. Because of this, you could not be forgiven for saying you "did not to know."

Therefore, we should not have to learn from our own mistakes. Learning from our own mistakes is seen as learning the hard way. But we can learn from the mistakes of our friends, relatives, siblings and avoid them. When you make a mistake, it is not the end of the world. You can correct it and also use it as an example for others to learn from.

We lived together as big extended families. When you had no elder siblings, you would learn from older cousins, aunties, uncles and anyone who was older and more experienced than you. This also fostered respect for elders. Even from the people below your age, it was expected that you listen when they are being rebuked because you could still learn something in the message. In conclusion, we learned to listen to advice regardless of who was being corrected.

Food for thought

Have you been in a situation where learning from someone else's mistake or advice helped you avoid making the same mistake yourself?

Tingasiga tasiga entomi.

"Tingasiga does not miss a punch"
Tingasiga loopt geen klap mis
(Nederlandse uitdrukking: Nieuwsgierig aagje/Nieuwsgierig aagje uit Enkhuizen).

Tingasiga is a name used to describe someone who wants to be involved in everything. Someone who does not know when to stop, when to walk away from a situation, or to control themselves when they need to do so. Someone who cannot control their curiosity.

Entomi literally means a punch as made by a fist like in a fight.

A common story of *tingasiga* is told of a man who went to a social gathering with friends to socialise After a few hours, it was time to go home. Some of his friends went home but he stayed. Some friends who had just arrived at the party convinced him to stay and have some more drinks with them. They were telling interesting stories and he didn't want to miss them. He always wanted to be a part of everything! He failed to say no to them because he wanted to be involved in all the stories they were sharing. So, he stayed longer talking. After a while, he was tempted to drink some alcohol because the friends offered it to him and they were also drinking it. He eventually started arguing with others. He got involved in a fight with someone and was punched in the face. He ended up helpless with a black eye, a swollen face and bruises. If he had left when it was time to leave, he would have been sober enough and not end up in a fight.

Such failure to control oneself and not knowing when to stop and walk away can be seen in many other scenarios. It does not only stop at people having alcohol. If someone always wants to pick arguments with others and does not know when to stop arguing, they are likely to end up in many fights. Someone who wants to know everything about everyone and always wanting to stay around and listen to what others are saying is likely to end up in trouble. Such a person is also like *tingasiga*. This is similar to the saying in English that "curiosity killed the cat."

The common lesson is: always know when to stop. Know your limits and keep to them. Lacking self-control always gets one in trouble. My mother always said that *"Too much of anything is always bad"*. Even eating too much of your favourite food can cause you tummy pain. Therefore, know when to stop eating even when it is still sweet.

Can you identify some scenarios in your life when you have been too curious, or when you have been like *Tingasiga* and maybe ended up with negative consequences? I remember a time I was so engrossed in the party, enjoying the fun of talking with different people that I kept postponing the time to leave and go home. By the time I finally left, it was so late that I missed the last regular high-speed train by a few minutes! The night trains were only riding every 45 minutes, so I had to wait 45 minutes for the next train which moves so slowly stopping at every small town. In the end, it took me more than 2 hours to get home instead of the usual 50 minutes I would have taken if I had left the party on time. Oh I regretted the extra time I spent at that party.

Akati keinikwa kakiri kabisi.

"A small tree is bent while it's still fresh".
Een kleine boom wordt gebogen als hij nog jong is.
(Nederlandse uitdrukking: Men moet de boom buigen als hij nog jong is).

There are many variations of this saying. Some say "a tree is bent while it is still young" while others say "a stick is bent while it is still raw/fresh"

In Tanzania they say in Swahili that "*Samaki mkunje akiwa bado mbichi, akishakauka hakunjiki.*" Which means that bend a fish while it is still raw and fresh out of the water, when it dries, it will not bend.

All these teach the same lesson.

This saying is from the background of places where farmers grew a lot of coffee. A coffee plant is bent and pegged to the ground in its early stages of growth. This enables it to produce more buds. This can only be done before the coffee tree matures. When the plant grows older, it hardens and becomes hard to bend. When you try to force it to bend, it will break and die. Likewise, if you try to bend any stick when it is fresh, it will bend easily. But once it is dry, it can only snap and break.

However, this proverb had a hidden meaning. It was focused on behaviour and disciplining a child. It meant that for one to shape the character of their children through discipline, it must be done when they are still young. Behaviour can easily be changed in the formative years of a person's growth. When the children are older and approaching teenage years, correcting behaviour becomes hard work both for the adult and the child. It is no longer automatic that they follow guidance. It is at this stage that adults and children's relations begin to get sour. The defiant and rebellious behaviour of adolescence starts. Although it is a normal part of development, if character was not formed earlier in life, there is a risk of broken relations at this point. In the Bible, a book for Christians, the part on *Proverbs:22:6*, also emphasises this proverb. It says: *"Train up a child on the way they should go and even when they are old they will not depart from it."* Whenever our parents needed to punish us, which was called *"okuhana"*, they did it with more emphasis, quoting this proverb. They wanted to make sure we knew what was expected of us. They also wanted us to understand that it was for our own good.

It is similar the common saying *"spare the rod and spoil the child"*. This meant that do not be afraid to correct your children. If you don't correct their behaviour when they are young, you will spoil them. Many people mistakenly understand the rod to be a physical stick that is used in physical punishments. That is not the true meaning. The rod can be any method used to encourage good behaviour and discourage bad behaviour. There are many punishment free ways of raising disciplined children. The more you know and use them, the higher the chance of raising happy and confident children who are not spoilt.

Parents wanted us to understand that they punished us because they loved us. They punished us because they wanted us to have a good future. That was hard to understand when we were feeling the pain of the punishment. As children, we though our parents were strict and harsh. But as we grew up, we realised it was done in love and we are better people because we received the guidance.

When we were growing up, guiding and correcting children was done communally. It was done by all elders. It was not the responsibility of the parents alone. All elders in the community whether your parent, relative or even nonrelatives were involved. If any of them found you involved in wrongdoing anywhere, they were free to correct you. This was because if any member of the community was not behaving well, the whole community felt the pain, not just the parents. Therefore, children generally followed the rules whether their parents are around or not. That is why the saying that "it takes a village to raise a child" was commonly used.

Showing children the right way to behave is one of the best gifts a parent can offer to them. This is a way of preparing them for the future. It is better than the most expensive toys you can give. Decently punishing your child does not mean that you hate them or do not like them but a way of shaping them for future good life. Some parents remember to parent their children at an older age when it's too late to control them. If the children do not learn the values necessary to live harmoniously in a society, they may fail to live well with others. This can lead to their unhappiness and failing in life as adults.

I will share a true-life story comparing two parents from two families with different parenting styles. This is a true story There were two brothers from the same family. Zacharia (not real names) and Butembere (also not real names) They grew up together. They both later married and started their own families. The family of Zacharia had 6 children while Butembere had 9.

While growing up, the children of Zacharia always thought their mother was the toughest. But she was also the most interesting woman in the village. Although she was tough, she would also show them that she really loved and cared for them. She would punish them in one moment, and in another moment, they would be having fun together as a family. She was bending them at an early age.

On the other hand, Butembere's wife used to talk badly about Zacharia's wife. She said that that she tortures her children and doesn't let them do what they want. Meanwhile no one would correct or even punish the Butembere children because the mother would complain if they did. She used to say that they were still too young to be punished, and that they would learn later when they grew up. They could do whatever they wanted, when they wanted. They had no boundaries at all. Years passed by, and children of both families grew up into big boys and girls. The results of the two families was very different.

Zacharia's family, with their "strict bad mum" were raised in a decent way. They studied well and all successfully completed their studies well through university. They had a god life, were happy with stable jobs and good incomes.

On the other hand, the children of the family of Butembere was the opposite story. None of the 9 children was able to finish secondary school. They struggled with keeping up with the discipline required to stay in school and study. Some of them dropped out at primary level and they turned out to be thieves. They even stole their father's property and sold it for money. They then spent all the money and were poor again. They could not work for anyone because they didn't listen to anyone. The girls got married at a very early age and struggled through life and poverty.

All this was not because one family was brighter or richer than the other. It is only because the children of Zacharia family had good **parental guidance** while the children of Butembere had **"parental pampering"** which is also **irresponsible parenting.** Therefore, it is every parent's responsibility to take care of their child and shape their morals and character while they are still young. It is also the responsibility of children to listen to parental guidance and correction. Failure of any of the two to perform their roles, the future of the family is at stake.=

Ekyokunda nikikunagisa ekyokweise.

"What you love can make you throw away what you already have"
Wat je begeert kan ervoor zorgen dat je weggooit wat je al bezit
(Nederlandse uitdrukking: Beter 1 vogel in de hand dan 10 in de lucht/Geen oude schoenen weggooien voor men nieuwe heeft)

This proverb basically means that what you like but do not yet have, can make you lose what you already have in your possession. Usually, we want things because we believe having them will make us happy. When we get what we want, we feel successful. We soon forget how badly we wanted them. We can even take having them for granted.

This is very easy to see with babies. When they have a toy in their hands and they see something they like, they immediately drop that toy and go for the other toy. This impulsive behaviour is normal in babies. As we grow older, it is expected that we become less impulsive and think more about the choices we make. Before we throw away what we have to go after what we desire, we must think first if it is worth losing it.

There are many examples of this. Sometimes we put so much effort in making a new friend that we forget or even ignore the friends we already have. At times when we are so angry at not getting a certain toy that we want that we forget to appreciate the good toys that we already have.

Parents also need to use this advice. Sometimes we want to make money so much that we work too much and forget our family. Family is what we have, we should not throw it away for any other desires.

Another common example is how people have been driven so much by economic development that they have forgotten the cost on the environment. Because people are buying too many things, most of what they don't really need, factories are making more to make everyone happy. As a result, the owners of big businesses are expanding and cutting trees to build more factories, using a lot of fuel in these factories, and producing a lot of waste. Sometimes they are dumping the waste in the wrong places like oceans. In the end, the earth, which is our home, the only home we have for now, is being destroyed. Every time you feel like you want to buy one more thing, ask yourself if you really need it. The less we all buy, the less the factories have to make. We can also think of reusing and recycling things. We don't want to risk losing our home, mother earth, because of being wasteful and wanting too much.

The Baganda people in Central Uganda have a saying that "*kyogala kikuseeza.*" This means that you can pay an unusually high price for something simply because you love it so much.

This advice is along the same lines as the common English saying that "*a bird in hand is better than two in the bush.*" What you already have is better than what you are yet to get. This does not mean you forget about trying to achieve more. It just means do not lose what you already have in the process of going after what you want. Therefore, this saying is a warning of sorts. Don't be too focused on getting what you want that you forget to count the high cost of getting it.

Akamanyiro nikarugamu akajogano.

Familiarity results in contempt
Vertrouwdheid resulteert in minachting
(Nederlandse uitdrukking: van genegenheid komt ook afkeer)

If someone (especially a child) becomes too familiar with you, that person may end up disrespecting you. In the African traditions and culture, there is a clear distinction between adults and children. There are generally accepted ways children should behave and interact with adults. It is based on respect and sometimes even fear.

Simple rules for children

1. Do not to talk back to adults when they correct you
2. Always greet adults
3. Children should not send adults on errands.
4. Children must not expect the adult to do things for them.
5. Children do not call adults by name.
6. Children should not hang around adults to listen to their conversations. And many more you will learn as you interact more with people of the different African cultures.

Following these simple rules was a sign of respect for elders. With respect to rule number 5, males were called "uncle" or "tata" which meant daddy. Tata was what you called the uncles that were siblings to your father. Elderly men were called "shwenhuru" which means grandpa.

Likewise, females were either auntie or "mama" or "nyakwenkuru" or "mukaka" both which mean grandma. Of course, different tribes have different equivalent names. But what is common is that adults were called by their titles, and not by their names.

Adults in turn demanded this respect and did not expect children to be so close to them. When they were engaged in discussion, children were expected to go away and play out of earshot. A child who wanted to be so close with adults and befriend them as if they were grown up was frowned upon. This was considered to be a sign of familiarity. A child who hung around adults curious of what they were talking about was frowned upon. It was feared that such a child will become disrespectful and begin to think they are at the same level with adults. Then they may begin to show signs of disrespect. That was not acceptable.

Adults were also expected to maintain this clear boundary and not encourage children to get used to being so close to them. For example, if you let a child get so close, they may begin to call you by name and that is not acceptable. There were also clear guidelines and boundaries to help adults know how to behave among themselves. For example, elders and bosses were given a level of respect that they were called by their titles and not by names. Wives were not allowed to call their fathers and mothers in law by name. They could call them "Mzee" which was a respectful title that meant old man.

Generally when I was growing up, I remember many people called my father by titles like *"Taata Gift"* which meant father of Gift(that's me);

"*director*" because he was a director at his job, others called him "*collector*" because he worked with the customs office and later they called him "Mzee Kyalimanya" because that was the name of his company. Rarely did I hear anyone call him George except his very close friends. This shows that people were generally called by their titles as a sign of respect. Women were called "*Maama....*" followed generally by the name of their first child. So my mother was generally called "*Maama Gift*" because I was her first child.

This tradition of not calling adults by name can cause some problems for a child born of parents from Uganda or Africa in general but growing up in Europe. In Europe children call their elders by name. They even talk back to parents as a way of voicing their opinions. Their parents of African descent can be very upset with the children for talking back as they find this very rude. Especially arguing back. Likewise, the parents find it challenging to understand why children answer back. Such a child can be confused because they have to be humble at home and talk back when they are with their multicultural counterparts. It is common to hear some parents say that "children raised in Europe have no respect!" But this is not really true, it is just a cultural difference.

In a similar light, adults who are educated in Africa and come to work or study in Europe find it a challenge that everyone voices their opinions freely when talking to bosses or senior colleagues. They may tend to be quieter or reserved. Those who seem shy could be considered as not proactive or not competent at work. On the other hand, when you work with an African boss, you could come across as rude or disrespectful simply for voicing your opinions at work.

How do you know when to talk and when to be quiet? In a situation where you are not sure of protocols or how to respond to others, just follow the guidelines of respect. Study and observe the working culture. And then act accordingly. This is because for some people, getting close may be considered familiarity and may fear that you will forget to respect them. In any case, there is no need to waste time complaining about the other's culture. You probably cannot change them, and they cannot change you. But you can certainly work well together once you understand that we are all raised differently.

A typical homestead showing everyone busy with their age appropriate tasks

CHAPTER 3:

RESPONSIBILITY/ HARD WORK

The four sayings in this chapter taught me the value of working hard on my chores. Children were expected to plan well and take their responsibilities seriously. I learned that when each person does their task well, everyone is happy because the job is complete.

Tokagira embwa okamoka.

You should not bark for yourself when you own a dog.
Je moet niet zelf blaffen als je een hond hebt
(Nederlandse uitdrukking: Niet alles zelf willen doen).

In the olden days in Africa, the main job of a dog was to guard a home. It did this by barking when it sensed a strange presence around the home. This could be a stranger like a thief or even a wild animal. This alerted the owners of the home to take care and look out. So, this proverb was formulated based on the "dog-owner relationship". A person who purposely bought a dog to protect him should not bark for himself. Once you have a dog, you do not have to bark for yourself.

Disclaimer!

I added this disclaimer after a conversation with a French friend of mine, He brought to my attention how this proverb can be grossly misunderstood by those who may interpret it as being cruel to children by equating them to dogs; or by thinking that children's tasks were of lower class or importance than adults' ones; or even by thinking that children were born for the sole purpose of doing tasks for their parents. Thank you, Sylvain, for this wonderful piece of insight.

I think this was my mother's favourite saying because she used it a lot. She was telling us indirectly that she cannot give birth to us, take care of us, raise us and still do most of the house chores. Our elders wanted to show us our responsibilities as children so that we could know what is expected of us and do it without complaining. Adults were not expected to do kids jobs, except when kids were not available to do them.

African families were generally large extended families. An extended family had children of different ages including cousins and younger aunties. Tasks were divided and there were chores for children at every age. Therefore, each child was expected to do their chores. For example, younger children did tasks like cleaning the house, compound gardening, washing dishes, fetching water from the well, herding the animals. Older children had tasks like cooking, looking after and teaching younger ones, working in the fields and many more. When children did their tasks well, the adults/parents had more free time to work on more complex tasks and plan for the family.

This was a very important way people naturally learned to do the activities of daily living. It was a kind of informal education passed on from generation to generation by age. There was no school where people learned to be self-sufficient and run a home. It was all done within the structure of the family setting and community. This was the basis of the belief that *"it takes a village to raise a child" and "charity begins at home"*:

Below is an example of some of the different tasks for different ages. This is adjusted for modern times so chores maybe different from the days when I was growing up. It gives an idea of how people in a home can divide the tasks depending on the ages and abilities of each person. This is demonstrated using the chores list for my two children aged 7 and 10 years. The family members meet often to redefine these tasks. Each child writing them down and keeping them where they can see them ensures that they constantly practice them till it is part of their routine. Gradually, adults did not need to be around to supervise these tasks. Older children helped supervise younger ones.

Chores for Kayla (6-9 years)

- make the bed ♥
- make the dinner tabble ★
- sweep the floor ♥
- qean up my room (toys on the floor) ♥★
- help clean up the yard ♥
- fold laundry ♥
- help empty dish washer ★
- wipe bathrooms, Kitchen, window ♥
- help cook (wash, find ingredients) ★

A child's handwritten list of home chores

Mython's chores (9 - 11 years)

- Vacum
- Mop floor
- Off - Load dish-washer
- clear the table after a meal
- do laundry
- make the bed
- take out the trash
- Suppurvise Kayla
- wash car
- help cook
- Help cooking (cut vegetables, help mesure.)

Hand made list of a child's home chores

Besides this labour division, there were some basic unsaid rules as below. We all knew them and automatically followed them. For example:

➢ It was not expected for an adult to be working while a child is doing nothing.
➢ An adult could send a child to do a chore or errand anytime. This could include sending them to the shop to buy things like sugar, salt, onions etc.
➢ As children, we were raised to be helpers of our parents and other adults.
➢ Every child knew their position and responsibilities in the family.

In line with this, children showed respect to elders or parents in many ways like below:

1. A child always greeted the adults.
2. A child helped to find a seat for an adult.
3. A child would not remain seated when an older person is standing, the child was expected to offer his seat to the elder person.
4. A child would help when they see an adult struggling with something like carrying a heavy bag of groceries, cleaning, etc
5. When sent, a child was expected to act immediately, not linger around playing. The child could certainly not refuse to be sent.
6. A child could not send an adult to do something for him. That was considered laziness. For example, a child could not say to the mother "please bring me my shoes" unless they were ill and unable to do it themselves.

All these and many others were seen a sign of responsibility by children not as burden put on them by the elders. It prepared them for the future life of personal responsibility.

Food for thought

What tasks do you have at home? Does everyone help or is it always the parents? If you are not helping already, think about what you could do to help.

Abateeki bingi nibasheisha emboga

Too many cooks spoil the broth
Te veel koks verpesten de soep
(Nederlandse uitdrukking: Veel koks bederven de brij)

Broth is a kind of thick soup. It is made by boiling different ingredients like vegetables or meat together in a good balance. If this is not done well, you can spoil the result. This proverb is basically trying to show that if many people try to give instructions on the same activity they may end up messing It up. Everyone will give their own ideas and make sure they work. In the end, this can be confusing for everyone and can result in wasted effort and a bad result.

This picture was drawn by my daughter Kayla (Then 6 years old) when I asked her what she understood from the proverb of too many cooks spoil the broth..

A story is told of a group of men and women who formed a catering group to prepare meals at parties. They made a good menu and divided the work amongst them. However, many of them wanted to make the beef stew because it was easy to make, and the stew is an important part of the meal. Since a lot of it was needed it was agreed that 3 of them will cook it. So, three men and one woman were in charge of preparing beef stew that day. They started cooking and soon were arguing about what type and amount of ingredients and spices to put in the pot. Each one had a different idea of what to use. Each though their idea was the best and was not willing to listen to the others. After a few arguments, each one secretly decided to add a little of their preferred spices. Two of them added salt in the sauce without tasting or asking each other if they had already put salt. In the end, the salt was too much, the spices were too much and out of balance, and the taste was terrible. That became a major disaster since beef stew was the main sauce for the meal. Literally speaking, "*too many cooks spoilt the soup*" that day. The lesson here is that if you are cooking something with someone, never add salt or other ingredients before tasting the dish or asking the other person if they have already added it. When working as a group, always agree on one way to do a task and stick to it.

We need to understand that for every project, one person has to take the lead in making the decisions. Even if you may feel that they are not as good as you are, you must listen to the leader for the sake of the success of the task. If too many people give instructions, it will lead to others being confused.

There is a similar saying that *"**Endimi nyingi zitukuruza obushera.-Too many languages spoil the porridge.** It gives the same advice

Osasire niwe ayara.

The one who is tired should make the bed (to sleep)
Degene die moe is moet het bed opmaken (om in te slapen)

This proverb in layman's language means that a person who is more in need of something should act first to make it happen. It was explained in a form of a making the bed to sleep. *"osasire niwe ayara"* means whoever is tired makes the bed, or lays the bed to sleep. This proverb was mostly used by our parents to teach us to be responsible for ourselves, to be independent. We needed to understand that we do mostly benefits us and not other people. If you do not take care of yourself well, nobody will do it for you. We shouldn't wait for others to do something for us. We can do things ourselves.

If you are hungry, you can do something about it by getting up and getting yourself something to eat! Doing something about is different from sitting on the table or chair and complaining to everyone that you are hungry. If you want to drink milk and there is none in the fridge, do something about it. Don't just complain about it. Action must always begin with you who is in need.

Grooming children this way helps them to grow up as responsible and independent persons who are focused on creating solutions to their own problems. Normally such people also become good at helping solve other people's problems.

Doing this makes you feel confident that you can always help yourself.

Embura omukoro nebagara obushaza.

"A person with nothing to do (idle person) weeds a garden of peas".

Iemand die niets te doen heeft (een lui persoon) wiedt een tuin vol erwten.
(Nederlandse uitdrukking: Wie niets omhanden heeft, haalt het onkruid tussen de bonen weg)
(An idle mind is a devil's workshop: Ledigheid is des duivels oorkussen)

Embura mukoro means an idle person or a person who has nothing to do. In the Banyankole-Bakiga culture, a farmer did not need to weed a garden of peas. Peas grew just as well amongst weeds. So, anyone who would be found weeding such a garden would be considered as idle. Weeding a garden of peas was a waste of time.

However, just like any other proverb, it has a deeper meaning than just weeding peas. Just as a saying goes, *"an idle mind is a devil's workshop."* This proverb points out the negative effects of being idle. When you have nothing to do, you are capable of getting strange ideas that can include doing what you are not allowed to do. You could even do things that get you in trouble.

As we grew up, our parents would tell us this to discourage us from being idle. They tried to keep us engaged at all times. More so, we did our allocated chores in time not to be called *"embura mukoro"* which was more of a shame to us as children. When we invented funny games, adults also teased us by saying we were idle.

In today's busy life, parents are always busy working. It means some children can grow up without enough parental guidance. The best gift you can ever offer to your child, is teaching them how to work or get involved in any kind of good activities. When children are idle and at home a lot with or without their parents, they end up spending too much time watching television; playing computer games or doing things they would not be allowed to do. They are more likely to get in trouble as they look up ways to entertain themselves. Also, a bored child starts to make unreasonable demands. It is important to have enough materials to play with as this can stimulate development. When bored, think of what you can do, or what you can create or plan. You can also find a friend and play interactive games together.

My parents always said this to us when we got involved in mischief as a result of being bored. "Find something good to do to keep you busy or else, evil will take up your mind." If you were seated around doing nothing, the adults asked you to find something to do or go outside and play.

Food for thought

Can you think of activities, games, or little projects that you can do in your free play time that do not involve watching TV or being on the computer, phone or tablet? Also think of those activities that you can do yourself that need no parental involvement or money. This list is actually endless. But it takes some creativity. As a fun exercise, make the list here below. If possible, also include if you can do this alone or with someone like a friend or sibling. If you can come up with 10 things, then you are not only a smart person but also very lucky.

Things to do in my free play time

1. _____
2. _____
3. _____
4. _____
5. _____
6. _____
7. _____
8. _____
9. _____
10. _____
    _____

Obwongo obunafu niburusya amaguru

"A lazy brain tires the legs".
Een lui brein vermoeit de benen
(Bezint eer ge begint)

This saying is all about planning ahead and thinking before taking action. Some tribes would say "A small brain tires the legs" while others even said "a small head tires the legs". They all meant the same thing

If you are too lazy to think or plan a project, you could end up spending more time on it because you may keep making mistakes. Correcting those mistakes can take time and get you very tired.

Imagine wanting to bake a cake. Planning properly involves making a list of what you need, then checking that you have everything before you start to bake. Before going shopping, it may be best to make a list of what you need. If you don't make the list, you may end up buying things you don't need, or forgetting things you need. Then you may get home to make your cake and realise that you have no eggs! You then have to go back and get eggs. Now you are making a double journey to the supermarket! Your legs will pay the price of your laziness in planning.

This applies in everything we have to do in life. Thinking logically and planning well are both signs that one's brain is not lazy. Failing to do that can mean that you waste time, use more physical effort than would be necessary. You can waste money spending on parts of a project that are not necessary. You may make many mistakes that need to be corrected costing you more time or money. This forms the very meaning of *"tiring the legs!"*

Therefore, always spend some good moments of thinking and planning. It saves you a lot and you can do much more.

Children suffer the consequences when parents fight

CHAPTER 4:

LOVE AND GOOD HEALTH

This chapter has my favorite sayings about living a good life. Our elders taught us to pay attention to the quality of life that we live. You will discover my grandfather's favourite saying.in this chapter.

Enjojo eibiri zarwaana, ebinyansi nibyo biri kubonaboona.

When two elephants fight, it is the grass that suffers
Waar twee olifanten vechten, lijdt het gras het meest
(De onschuldige derde)

two African bull elephants fighting

This saying brings to attention the fact that the consequences of one's actions can affect more than just the people involved.

Naturally, an elephant is a huge animal. An adult African elephant can weigh 2,268 to 6,350 kilograms. Wherever it steps, the ground feels its weight. In a fight, 2 elephants are bound to destroy anything they step on. Small animals can run off and hide but grass is unable to move so it suffers the most. However, the grass is innocent and is not involved in the fight. This grass symbolises the innocent people affected. Our great forefathers developed this saying with a picture, at the back of their minds, of two powerful people fighting one another while innocent people suffer the consequences.

This also applies in our day to day lives as human beings. In many bad situations, there is always innocent victims. One example is when there is hostility in a home where parents are fighting or having disagreements often. It is usually the innocent children that suffer. This suffering can be directly visible emotional trauma of the children, neglect and lack of basic needs or being abandoned by either side of the parents. Sometimes it can be mental and psychological trauma of the children seeing their parents fight. In worst cases, children maybe wrongly punished because the parents are angry with each other. This is displacement. It happens when one party feels powerless to punish the partner and transfers their anger to a powerless innocent victim like a child.

A second example is when there a war which is usually due to poor leadership in any community. The civilians who are not involved in the war feel the bad effects more than even the ones who started the war. Usually innocent women and children are affected. They may fail to get food, water, medicines. Sometimes they are forced to leave their homes and property to live somewhere else as refugees.

In another example, political leaders of different parties may disagree with each other. Then one party may misuse their power and pass laws which are intended to punish the other group. These may turn out to be very unfair to their common citizens who are just living their normal life and are not involved in the disagreements.

Another example is, when workers in any organisation go on strike protesting unfair pay or conditions by employers, government or worker's unions. It is usually people receiving their services who suffer because they are not being served. When I was at university, the teachers normally went on industrial action (also called a strike), because they were not paid well. When this happened, we missed lessons and study hours. This could go on for days or weeks if the two parties did not come to an agreement. As a result, privately sponsored students who had to pay their own tuition fees and also accommodation suffered the most. This is because they would have to incur unplanned costs when the term got extended or we all missed valuable education hours that we could not recover. Sometimes this led these students to also go on a strike. But the students were innocent, the fight was between the teachers and the university!

Therefore, every time you think of doing anything unpleasant to someone else, think of the innocent people that maybe affected by your actions. Try to find a solution or a way where no innocent people are affected.

Amagara nigakira amagana

Having a healthy life is better than having a lot of riches.
Een goed leven is meer waard dan rijkdom
(Nederlandse uitdrukking: Gezondheid is niet te koop).

Amagara means good health or in some cases life.
Amagana means hundreds which can be translated to having plenty of something or even lots of money.

This answers the question: Is it better to have life (good health) or plenty of money/riches? This also includes being famous because many people equate being famous to being rich. In Africa it was generally believed that it is best to have good life and good health. Having life could also be interpreted in many other ways, like being wise, being surrounded by loving family, having many true and caring friends.

This is the biggest lesson elders emphasised. Be careful not to spend too much time accumulating wealth (like money, toys, properties), at the expense of your health, peace of mind, family and friendships. This is especially if doing this disconnects you from forming good family bonds and community relations. You gain nothing if you get lots of wealth but lose the love and time with your family.

Learning this early in life is important in today's world when there is so much competition. The cost of living is high and people have to work such long hours to make a good life. The cost and definition of what it takes to make a good life keeps changing making it hard to attain with satisfaction. When you feel stretched, remember that *"Amagara nigakira amagana"*

This saying has a lot of wisdom and many interpretations. During friends' arguments, fights and conflicts where each one tries to convince the other that their views are the right ones, my grandmother also always said that *"it is better to be happy than to be right"*. She said this when I could not let go of an argument, when I felt that I had to win the argument at all costs. She would say to me, "maybe you win the argument, but you could lose a friend." What is more important? That you were right, or that you are both happy without getting into a fight? Is it not better that you have maintained peace with each other? It is better to be happy and at peace than to be right.

As I grow older, I understand what she meant. I realise that it is better to be happy. I know now that I don't have to be "right" all the time, so I let things go easily. I find that I am much happier. Things don't bother me as much as they used to.

People sacrifice a lot to get what they want. Every time you feel you are losing touch with life or friends, remember, *amagra nigakira amagana*. It is better to have life than having plenty of whatever is causing you to disconnect from family.

A point of caution here is not to say that Africans discouraged prosperity. On the contrary, communal prosperity was encouraged. As long as there was a balance. Everything good was encouraged in moderation.

Kaabe kaakye kanure

Its better if its little but tasty
Het is beter als het klein maar smakelijk is
(Nederlandse uitdrukking: Het hoeft niet veel te zijn, als het maar lekker is)

This is like the English expression that *"less is more"* This was my grandfather's favourite saying. I cannot say it without remembering him and how he would tell us stories whenever he was in one of his happy moods. He was not a rich man, but he was always jolly. What we loved about him the most was that he was happy and contented with what he had. He used this saying a lot mainly in relation to food. He emphasized that it was best to have a small amount of food but well prepared and tasty than plenty but not appetising. The saying emphasised quality over quantity.

The hidden meaning is that it is better to have less and enjoy it with all your heart than to keep yearning and looking for more than you can have at the time. He always discouraged dissatisfaction among his children and grandchildren He considered these to be the source of greed. He taught us to be aware of the dangers that can result such as cheating, unhappiness, stealing, jealousy. These are all bad habits. Be content and you will avoid them.

This saying was a kind of warning. Emphasis was on having less wealth and being contented and happy, than having a lot of wealth and being unhappy. It was common that some people got a lot of wealth which turned out to be a problem instead of a blessing, while others lived happy lives without necessarily having a lot of wealth.

It therefore means that you can have little wealth, live a simple life and be happier than people who have a lot of wealth. Especially if the wealth is gotten by cheating or mismanaging others. Such people cannot have peace of mind or even be happy. Elders emphasised that life is not about the wealth you have accumulated but how you have got it, and how you relate with others after getting. Even when you have a lot, you should treat all people well.

Imagine what is better? Having plenty of toys most of which you don't even like or use? Or having a few that you love to use, value and share with loved ones?

The same can be said about friendships. It is better to have a few good friends whom you have close relations than so may friends that you don't even connect well. These days people have so many online friends but almost no real friends to connect with or talk to. Invest in making few but good solid friendships.

The same goes for clothes. Some people buy so many poor-quality clothes because they like to buy everything they see. The same amount of money can be used to buy fewer but better-quality clothes. It is better if it is little but tasty. Less is more.

Akitariho tikiriza omwana

'A child cannot cry for what is not there (What the child does not see, they do not cry for).

Een kind kan niet huilen om wat er niet is (wat het kind niet ziet) (wat je niet kent, dat mis je niet)

This is also like the English saying that *"out of sight is out of mind"*

Babies are very innocent human beings. If they don't see something, they cannot demand for it by crying. But if they can still see it, they will cry until they get it.

When a baby has something in their hands and the parent realises it's not good for them and takes it away, the child will begin to cry. However, if the child gets distracted, they will immediately stop crying and focus on something else. This means that the child has changed their focus from what they had before and is now looking what they have in front of them. In the same way, as we were growing up, we were taught through this proverb that we should never cry for what we do not have. We were not allowed to go around begging people who had something we liked.

In short, one should be contented with what one has and feel at peace with it. We can still be happy without certain things in life. Remove your eyes from what you want and focus on what you have. Enjoy it in full instead of crying for what you cannot get. Find ways to distract yourself if not having it is causing you to "cry".

One day we had to share some food that was so yummy, but my sister was in boarding school and I was feeling sad that she will miss the food. This is because the food in boarding school was not so tasty. So, we started to think of keeping for her, but the food would not last so long. My mother advised us not to worry so much because she did not know that we are eating and so she could not miss in the way we imagined. She would have to be content eating what the school served until the holidays when she would come home. Then maybe we would make a special meal for her.

When you want something so badly and are still not able to get it, take your attention away from being sad about it and focus on what you have. You can do this by taking time to enjoy and appreciate what you have; thinking about other things that make you happy. Really just do anything that distracts you from your sadness or any negative feeling about not having what you want.

Each individual stick is easy to break, but a bundle with all the sticks together is unbreakable!

CHAPTER 5:

UNITY/TEAMWORK

In this chapter is a collection of my favourite sayings about working together as a team. I learned that when more people put positive effort in a goal, it becomes easier to achieve.

Abangana tibakanya.

People who hate each other cannot multiply
Mensen die elkaar haten, kunnen zich niet vermenigvuldigen
(Johan Cruijff said: 'Alleen kan je niets, je moet het samen doen')

This proverb is common among the Banyakitara from Western Uganda. It literally means, when people in a community are divided, they cannot multiply. A community in this sense can be a group or team, family or housemates or workmates or a village. For any community to multiply in results or prosper, they must be united and work as one. They need to work together and not against each other.

Generally, people who don't like each other, cannot work well together, they cannot help each other, and as a result they cannot achieve a goal or produce good results. There is no unity in such a group. Everyone does what they feel is best for their lives without thinking about the needs and wishes of others. This community will have a lot of disagreements and conflicts. As a result, they cannot agree on matters for the common good. This can apply to jobs at work, or sports teams. But when a team works well together with mutual respect for each other's abilities, they are likely to have good results and succeed at anything they put their mind on..

In the olden days, a community had strength in numbers. People were safer living and working together in communities. They could grow enough food, protect their communities from outside enemies and multiply. The saying, *"united we stand, divided we fall."* resulted from the realisation of such strength in co-operation. In fact, the worst punishment for wrong doers was to chase them away from the community. Then they would be alone and unsafe.

In African tradition, unity in a family was very important. No matter what differences existed, family members had to stick together. Therefore, it was not expected to speak badly about a family member outside the family. This was because outsiders could use this opportunity as a weapon to divide the family. Family members protected each other, community members protected each other.

Growing up with siblings in large extended families tested the children's resolve to show unity. We had fights and conflicts over small things like toys, clothes, chores etc. But when we were away from home in the community, we looked out for each other and protected each other. We looked after our little sisters and brothers and forgot our fights. Families that worked together were great and prosperous while those that had quarrels remained struggling and could not move ahead.

My grandmother always reminded me of this need to love each other and stick together when I was angry with my parents or siblings. This was especially when I felt they were being annoying or disagreeable.

While growing up, I often heard similar religious saying that "A family that prays together, stays together". Some other people also often say that "A family that eats together grows together". All this emphasised the importance of keeping the family together in unity.

Religious books like the Bible and Quran emphasize unity as one way to bring believers together. *"Do two people walk together unless they have agreed to do so?"* **Amos 3:3.**

We were always told a story of a man who had 7 sons. He raised them well and taught them the value of love for each other. As he grew very old, he realized these seven had started having disagreements very often. He called all of them to a family meeting. As a tradition in most African societies, before a man died, he divided his possessions among all his sons. He also had to choose an heir to represent his interests in the family and community when he was gone. So, all his sons were curious to know what the meeting was about. Before the meeting started, he requested each of them to go to a nearby bush and bring two sticks the size of a small walking stick. They came back with two sticks each. The meeting started with this illustration.

He told each of them to pick one stick from the two they had brought and stand up with it. He instructed them, "Hold your stick and try to break it as many small parts as possible," he added. They did so and each of them was able to break the single stick easily broken pieces. Then he requested them to collect the other seven sticks together and tie them in a bundle. The old man instructed them thus, "Let each one of you try to break the bundle of the sticks." They all tried and even the strongest of them was not successful after so many attempts.

He then told them to listen very carefully as he explained his lesson to them. "That single stick you have broken is you as an individual. Alone you are easy to destroy. But the sticks in the bundle are all of you together, united as a family." He added, "Once you are separated from one another and you stay as an individual, you will be broken down easily and defeated by any problems in this life. But when you, my seven sons, stick together and unite, no force can defeat you. I have so many properties here on earth. But the most important I leave with you is love and unity my sons." he concluded. They were all amazed at the lesson their father had taught them. They reconciled and promised him that they would stick together and work well together. With this assurance, the father had no reason to divide his property among the them. He was assured they would do it themselves without conflict. He rested well believing that he had left a legacy of a united family capable of multiplying.

In conclusion, sometimes as an individual, you have to let go of your own desires in the interest of the group's common goals. Imagine in a (football) team, if each player wants to be the only one to individually shine, then he ignores the fact that other team members also have capability to contribute to the score. In the end the rest of the team gets annoyed with this selfishness and may fail to work as a team. Even if all players are individually excellent, if not organised and working together in co-operation, a weak team can easily win against them.

Ageteriine niigo gaata iguffa.

The teeth that come together can break a bone.
Tanden die samenwerken kunnen een bot breken
(Nederlandse uitdrukking: Vele handen maken licht werk)

This saying originates from the culture of people who like to eat meat with bones. The Ankole people like to eat meat with bones. I have come to realise many other people do. Some people, including myself, love to chew on the bone. Bones are not soft like the meat. One's teeth need to be strong enough to bite well. In cases where the bones are a little soft, we literally chew and eat them. However, one needs to have strong teeth, and use the biting teeth together. It is very difficult to eat meat off the bone using just one or two teeth alone, especially if the two or more teeth have wide gaps in between. All the teeth need to be used together to be effective. It was always particularly funny to try to eat the bone when one has lost the front teeth as happens between the ages of 5-8 years. One was said to have wide gaps called *"mapengo."* or "ebyaasha" A person with mapengo could not easily eat meat off bones.

The saying explains that a joint effort makes work easier. This is similar to the English saying that *"Many hands make light work"*

My grandmother commonly told us this in some scenarios like; when any of us was acting lazy and refusing to participate in group tasks or assignments, or when we seemed to be failing to agree on what to do. Always remember this when you are supposed to work together, and you feel like not helping; or when you realise that some people are not doing their fair share of the work. Also, when you feel lazy to get involved, please remember that your small effort counts a lot towards the whole group achieving the task. Only when you work together in a combined effort, you can accomplish the task, just like breaking the bone

Emitwe ebiri nekira gumwe.

Two heads are better than one
Twee hoofden zijn beter dan een

You may already guess that this does not really mean that a person is better off having two heads instead of one. The head in this case signifies the action of thinking. It means that when two people think together to find a solution to a problem, it will be easier to solve it. This is because each one brings new ideas and perspectives to help find the solution. Have you ever heard of the phrase *"let us put our heads together?"* It basically means let us think together and come up with solutions. This encourages people to seek advice when having difficulty.

Sometimes we want to do things alone or we find difficulty solving a problem alone. We may fear to ask for help because we don't want others to laugh at us. In such cases, don't be afraid to ask for help. Remember that two heads are better than one. Usually, as you think through a challenge with someone else, you may discover new thoughts and solutions that had not crossed your mind. There is a similar English expression that "A problem shared is a problem halved:"

Never be afraid to ask for help. Two heads are better than one

A word of caution here. Asking for help is different from talking about your problems with everyone who cares to listen. Only discuss your challenges with people whose opinions and advice you value, and who you believe can be a part of helping you find a solution. Otherwise it becomes a matter of depressing talk and you may end up sharing your problems with people who are either not interested or will get the chance to gossip about you and even add to your problems.

Above: a poorly prepared farmer may never finish the day's job on time.
Below: A well prepared farmer achieves much more in a shorter time and the results are more impressive

CHAPTER 6:

BRAVERY/COURAGE.

This chapter is a collection of the memorable sayings that taught me to be brave and approach every situation with courage.

Owamaani takyeera.

A person with strength does not rush to be early.
Iemand met kracht haast zich niet om op tijd te zijn

Amaani in this case can mean strength, skill or energy. *Owamani* is someone who has these qualities

Okukyeera means to be up early. It can also mean being earlier than expected.

This saying has its origins from one of the hard-working tribes of people in South Western Uganda called **Bakiga.** The Bakiga people majorly occupied the districts of Kabale, Kanungu and Rukungiri. They were popularly known for being physically strong and hardworking. Despite their physical strength and hardworking nature, they realised that success was not all about waking up so early and using physical strength. It was also about other aspects like proper planning and determination which were aspects related to mental capacity rather than determination But because the Bakiga people are generally physically strong and energetic, most people misunderstand this proverb to mean that it emphasizes physical strength above all else.

This proverb aimed to highlight other good qualities that someone needs to have apart from physical strength. In fact, it suggests that someone with these qualities, even if less physically strong, can perform better than one without them.

Owamaani could describe someone with strong attributes that put him at an advantage compared to one without them. So, owamani can be described as someone who:

- ✓ is skilled
- ✓ plans well
- ✓ Is clever or enterprising
- ✓ Is organised
- ✓ Is courageous

Someone without the above values could end up wasting time and therefore taking longer to accomplish a task, even if they are physically strong and energetic. These attributes give one a kind of head start that physical strength alone cannot give.

Sometimes the Bakiga used this saying to encourage themselves. If someone woke up late but had to go to the garden to dig, knowing this proverb would keep them motivated believing that even if they came later, they could still accomplish the day's job if they worked hard and consistently.

In modern times, this teaches us that at any stage in life, you can begin a new phase. This can be a new career. It does not matter which age you are, what you have gone through, or what others who started before you have already done What matters is a determined, courageous and brave mind to get up and begin going in the direction you want. You can will always get there eventually.

It therefore means that you must know the qualities that set you apart and also the weaknesses that slow you down. Knowing these well, you can focus on things that bring out your best strengths but also gradually work on those aspects where you are likely to struggle. It is said you can make up in skill what you lack in strength. For people who do marketing, you make up in numbers what you lack in skill.

Imagine you are generally not good in something; you may make up that weakness by putting in more than the average hours in practice. All is possible to a determined mind. What are you determined to achieve? Where do you have to put more focus? Make a good plan, and you are on your way to success. It is just a matter of time.

Owarumirew enjoka atiina omwiina

He who was bitten by a snake fears a hole.
Wie gebeten is door een slang, is bang voor een hol

Snakes are known to live in holes. So, someone who has been bitten by a snake fears any hole they see. Even just the sight of a hole can bring fear because it is a reminder that there is possibly a snake. In fact, the sight of anything that may look like a snake can bring fear for example a lizard. Although they may look similar, one is dangerous while the other is not. We know that there are many other small animals that live in holes. In fact, holes for different animals can look different like the holes below.

And a hole for a snake

A hole of an armadillo

A hole for a bird in a tree

A hole in on a tree

A hole that is a home for a rodent

So, you can see that not every hole has a snake in it. This proverb was talking about being too cautious. It advises us to be cautious but not to extremes. In fact, being too cautious can mean that you end up not doing anything because of fear.

There is a similar English saying, "*once bitten, twice shy*". A friend also used to say "Fool *me once, shame on you, but fool me twice, shame on me*". This means you can avoid making the same mistake twice by being cautious. So, we need to be cautious enough not to be fooled twice but be brave enough to try again. Many people fail to do things because they fear that they will fail. This is especially if they have tried it before and failed. Or if anyone they know has tried before and failed.

The fact that we fail once does not mean we shall fail again. We can have the courage to try again. Being cautious means, we look at all possibilities to prevent ourselves from making the same mistake. It does not mean we fear to try altogether.

In each case, situations can always be different. Therefore, look at and judge each situation separately, and then take your chance. Not every hole has a snake.

Eryarebekire tiryita efuka.

The stone that you can already see does not damage the hoe.

De steen die je kunt zien zal de schoffel niet beschadigen.

This is my favourite saying on the subject of being brave. Knowing this saying gives me courage and confidence.

The people of Western Uganda are farmers. To them, a hoe was instrumental in every home. It was valuable as it was used in gardening. A hoe is a long-handled gardening tool with a thin metal blade, used mainly for weeding and loosening soil before planting seeds. It is treated with care and should not be damaged by knocking it against hard objects like stones. Digging in a stony, rocky garden is not good because those stones can damage the hoe. Once it is damaged, it becomes blunt and will not work properly anymore. That can be a big loss. The hoe then must be repaired or replaced. This can cost a lot of money. Therefore, all care is taken to make sure the hoe is not damaged.

One has to always dig carefully because some stones can be hidden under the soil, especially when you need to dig deep. Some stones were so large or hard that the hoe can break! But this proverb says that a stone that has already been seen cannot damage the hoe. Once you have seen it, it is no longer the danger because you can carefully remove it or dig carefully around it. You should only worry about the stone that is still covered by soil, that which you have not seen.

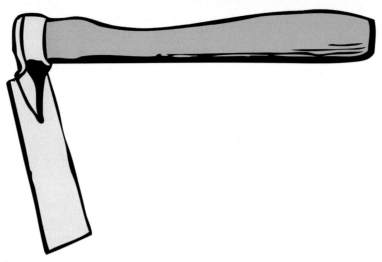

The typical hoe has a strong and sharp metal edge with a long wooden handle.

As you can imagine, this saying had a hidden meaning, more than stones damaging hoes. Day to day life exposes us to challenges all the time. Some are anticipated, others are completely unexpected. Some are brought by our own weaknesses, our friends, family and loved ones, while others can also be by work or study situations. These challenges are part of life like the stones are part of the garden. This proverb explains that once you see and know these challenge or weakness, then they can no longer harm you or put you down. Just like an English proverb that says, *"fore-warned is fore-armed"*, you are then more prepared knowing what you are up against.

This was basically to empower us as children to know that when you have identified your problem, then it is easy to take care of it or even avoid it. Therefore, no need to be afraid of it, just figure out the best way to face it or remove it. I find this really empowering.

Imagine you find out that there is a bully in your school and you even know who it is. You are then less afraid because now that you know who it is and the method they use to bully. You can either plan to avoid them or be strong enough not to be affected by their bullying method. You can even look up ways on "how to deal with bullies" or ask an adult to advise you. In the end you want to be able to face the situation with confidence and no fear.

Another example is: Imagine you realise that the reason you are getting sick so often is because you are not eating enough healthy fruits and vegetables! Now you can plan on eating them regularly, even if it may be hard at first.

The big challenge is not knowing what the problem is, or where it is, or how it looks. Once you know, you are empowered. You can overcome it. It doesn't mean that it will be easy, but it will not frighten or disturb you as much. Knowledge is power. The stone that you can already see cannot damage the hoe.

Food for thought

Can you identify some situations when knowing something ahead of time has enabled you to have an easier time?

Ebya Ruhanga tobara n'enumi nezaara.

With God everything is possible, even a bull can give birth to a calf.
Met God is alles mogelijk, zelfs een stier kan een kalf baren

Ruhanga means God in Runyankole language. It can also be used to describe a higher power way above human understanding. This proverb was an extreme example to demonstrate that with God, even what is thought to be impossible can be possible. It seems extreme to think that a bull can give birth. In real life, this is something that is seen as impossible. Some things in life just look Impossible from a logical human perspective, simply because we have never seen them happen. This saying recognised the fact that even what we knew as possible could be limited by the human perspective. But for people who believed in a higher power, much greater than human power can understand, everything is possible. "God" in this case meant a supernatural high unexplained power to whom all things can be possible.

This saying was basically used by our parents to teach us never to give up, even when things looked impossible. It was all about having faith. This was a helpful reminder when things seemed impossible or completely out of reach. We were raised not to give up because things can always turn around. This reduced the element of doubt. It empowered us with courage to face anything.

For any person to attain success in anything in life, we must take a step of faith. That could mean, deciding to do something when you are not sure of the outcomes or the benefits. Life is more than what we see with our eyes, it's actually more of what we can believe to be or hope to have. The only thing to do is to take a step and begin the journey with the belief that it will be well. It is said that: *"Every journey of a thousand miles begins with a single step."* No journey begins at the finishing point It has to begin by taking a single step in the right direction. We have to BELIEVE that it is POSSIBLE even if the LOGICAL MIND tells us otherwise. This is because our fathers believed that the logical mind was limited in what it could see, but with faith in God we could achieve the unimaginable.

It takes a brave mind to make some choices in life. We always fear to take risks or make mistakes. We are afraid of possible unsolvable challenges ahead. Since we cannot see the future, our belief will lead us through the unknown. For nothing is impossible if we believe. *Even a bull can give birth to a calf*

Omugisha gw'enkoko tigwe gw'endahi.

The blessing (luck) of a chicken is not the same as that of a guinea fowl.
De zegen (het geluk) van een kip is niet hetzelfde als die van een parelhoen.

Omugisha means luck or blessing. In fact, my name Mugisha means exactly that. *Enkoko* is a chicken while *endahi* is a guinea fowl. Chickens and Guinea fowls look very similar, but yet chicken live with humans (domestic) while guinea fowls live in the bush (wild). They are both edible, but a chicken is more likely to end up at the dinner table than the guinea fowl. A guinea fowl has more freedom because it lives in the wild. This proverb teaches us to be aware that situations can seem the same but have very different outcomes.

Our parents often used this proverb to discourage us from comparing ourselves with other people based on what they had that we did not have. Although we may look the same, we are never the same. We may even have similar characteristics but cannot have the same circumstances in life. Comparisons were never encouraged by our parents, especially if it was about being sad about what we didn't have. They encouraged us that whenever you like something of someone else, work hard for it and achieve it by yourself. But if you don't get it, be happy with what you have. Life was not to be seen as unfair to some and fair to others. We all have different blessings. This compares to the common saying that "*The grass is always greener on the other side.*" Sometimes things may always seem easier or better for the other person, but you do not see or know what they had to do to be where they are.

In business, this also applies. Some cases we could take the same risk, but some people succeed while others don't. If someone tries something and fails, it should not discourage you from trying it for fear of the same failure. Your luck can be different, and circumstances are never the same.

This was always a reminder for us as children when we tried to follow someone's bad example. If someone does something naughty and does not get caught, don't automatically assume that you can do it and not get caught. In the end your luck may not be the same as their luck. Sometimes you are the chicken, other times you may be the guinea fowl. Be careful, be content, be happy with what you have.

a farm chicken

a guinea fowl

At meal times, if you lost your focus and started talking, your favourite food could be eaten by someone else.

CHAPTER 7:

FOCUS

This chapter has the great proverbs from which we learned to keep focus on a task, follow instructions and never give up.

Wasimagira nibabega.

If you lose focus, your food will be taken by others.
Als je niet oplet, zal een ander je eten afpakken

This was also used mostly by our great grandfather to teach us to keep focused all the time in what we were doing or where we were going. And more so it showed us the result of losing focus on what you are doing at any time could result in a loss. It was common when we were eating, especially on those special days we had meat. We were expected to focus on our plate because whenever you looked aside, someone could take your meat and eat it. Mealtimes were fun and communal because we used to eat from one big plate which we called *orusaniya"*. Whenever one lost focus and started playing around or talking, you could find all the food eaten and you may go hungry. Slow eaters had to be particularly focused and careful. Adults sometimes supervised the eating so that they could constantly remind the slow eaters to focus on eating and less talking. If you lost your attention on the eating, the rest continued to eat and finished the food. Eating well was important because mealtimes were fixed with no snacks in between. So, if you didn't eat well and were hungry later, you would have to wait for the next mealtime. This saying did not teach us to focus on food alone, but on whatever you are involved in at the moment.

I would like to share a story of when we were growing up in the village. It was dinner time and as usual we all sat on the mat to eat. It was a cheerful meal since it was a Saturday and our daddy had bought chicken. Everyone had been excited and could not wait for dinner time to taste the chicken stew. It would be served with rice and our favourite green banana called *matooke* steamed in banana leaves. Dinner was finally served! We all sat in a circle on the floor. We each got two pieces of chicken in stew served in our own individual small bowls. The *matooke* some rice was served on one big o*rusaniya* placed in the centre of the circle for all to share. We blessed the food with the usual short prayer and started eating. Initially, we all ate in silence still excited and enjoying the meal. Most of us ate the stew first with food, saving the pieces of chicken for last. Soon some people were less focused on their meals and started talking. One of my elder cousins seated next to me called out my name and said there was a cat behind me. Knowing that I was afraid of cats, she meant to trick me to take attention from my plate. I jumped out of fear turning back to the door to look at the cat which was actually not there. I accidentally knocked down the candle putting the whole room in darkness. At that point, everyone knew what to do, that is, to hold their plates in their hands to protect their chicken as they waited for mummy to light up the candle again. Of course, my plate was not protected as I was still running away from the imaginary cat and now it was dark. By the time light was back on, my plate was empty. Of course, I cried but it was too late because we had been warned about losing focus while eating. So, from that day, I learnt a lesson to always focus on my food or always eat my favourite part of the meal first. To date, no one has ever admitted to eating my piece of chicken. Mummy scolded everyone and told us not to trick anyone at mealtime again. But my chicken was gone forever! This is an extreme example, it may seem very unfair but I learned from it.

Another common example is when you are playing with something and you put it down to play with something else. It could be the TV remote when you have been watching something and you walk away to do something else. Another person can pick it up and play with it because it is free. You can't cry for it because it is assumed that you were 'done using it when you put it down' Therefore if you are still interested in something, keep it in your focus.

This really applies to everything in life. When you lose focus, other people continue to move forward, and they can as well take your chances. It means that when you lose focus, what you lose can never be recovered. Time is one example. Every minute you lose is lost forever. Therefore, one must use time productively and not waste it by doing unproductive things. Always stay focused on what you do.

Nyakazaana akerinza ogwarakore

"The servant procrastinates about his work, yet he knows he eventually has to do it"

"De knecht stelt zijn werk uit, maar hij weet dat hij het uiteindelijk toch moet doen
(Nederlandse uitdrukking: Het is slechts uitstel van executie/stel niet uit tot morgen, wat je vandaag kunt doen)."

Nyakazaana is derived from "omuzaana" which means a female servant/helper. This talks about someone who has specific tasks that they have to do. But due to laziness and continuous distractions, they keep putting off doing those tasks. However, in the end they still must finish them. Therefore, a focused person would not postpone their tasks but just start doing them, finish and can then relax. The work will not disappear even when they become lazy about it. In the end, when they realise that they cannot put it off any longer, they panic and rush through it and may not do it well.

An example:

Kapere is a boy who has a day off from school. He knows he must do homework to finish certain tasks in Maths, English and Science by 5pm. He also needs to clean up his room and prepare his sports clothes for gym the next school day. He finds some of these tasks boring and feels lazy to get started at all. First, he decides to watch some television. Two hours later he is still feeling lazy, he decides to play a computer video game. At about midday, he decides to browse the internet for some of his favourite music videos. He is getting lazier instead of getting started. But in the end, he is still the one to do the work. He asks his sister to help but she has her own tasks so she will not help him. By 3:00 pm, he realises he has only 2 hours to do everything he should have done in a whole day. He gets up, panics and starts on his tasks.

By now we can all guess how it ends. By 5:00 pm, he is only halfway. He ends up working till 7pm, his room is not well cleaned, and his parents are not happy with him and put away his computer game for a week.

The next time you feel lazy to start your tasks, think of Kapere's example. Don't procrastinate because in the end you still must do the job.

Below are some tips for Kapere and for you when you feel lazy in future:

1. write down your tasks: For example, math homework, english homework, science homework, clean my room, prepare my gym clothes, take a short break (rest a little), play.
2. start with the task you love more, but not the break or play because these are not tasks. This will energise you to carry on to the next tasks and before you know it, you will be finished in no time.
3. Plan the time for breaks in between so that you can do the fun things you like in between the tasks. If you don't plan, the fun things will take more time than the actual tasks.

4. Be realistic how much time each task can take. Imagine Kapere had only two hours to finish everything! That is not enough but he realized it too late!

<u>Food for thought</u>

Can you think of more tips? Do you remember moments when you have been like Kapere? Remember always, *Nyakazaana akerinza ogwarakore, and then get started*.

Owubasigire ati bandinzire.

"He who is being left behind, thinks they are waiting for him".
"Hij die achterblijft, denkt dat de anderen op hem wachten."

This proverb is priceless. Through it, our forefathers were really encouraging us to keep focused in whatever we do and not base our progress on others. Basing our progress on others can give you false hope that you are not alone because you do not know what they do when you are not with them.

As any normal children growing up, we were sometimes naughty or did things that we knew were not allowed. Sometimes we had more courage to do these things when we were with friends who were also doing the same. This is called peer pressure. It results in doing things you wouldn't do just to feel like you fit in or belong to a group. What we did not understand then, was that people can encourage you and even cheer you on to do wrong. But you face the consequences alone.

A person can cheer you on and support you in doing wrong but when consequences catch up with you, you face them alone. They may cheer you on but when you are caught or in trouble, they can also laugh at you or leave you alone to suffer. You have to be ready to take responsibility for your actions or mistakes and not just copy others just to fit in.

When my little brother was in high school, it was a boarding school for boys but they had some freedom to leave the school premises almost every day. Some of them could roam around nearby towns without adult supervision.

This was a new kind of freedom for most of them because in the primary boarding school, they were not allowed to leave without permission. But it was such a danger to some boys who had no self-control and could not resist the temptations by friends who constantly asked them to walk with them to the shops. Eventually, many were somehow dragged into many things like night discos in town, drinking alcohol in the nearby bars, all of which were not allowed. They formed many peer groups in school that had different rebellious nicknames. The notorious one was called *"kyangabukama"* (which means a group that refused to live by rules). Members of these peer groups planned and did such things together and had an agreement that they could not betray each other to the authorities in case any of them was caught. However, many got so busy enjoying themselves that they forgot that they were in school to study hard and pass their assignments. They forgot that they had different academic abilities. Some could play but also later focus on study. In the end, the final exam results always shocked them. Because while some failed, a few of their friends passed really well. Those who didn't do well could not believe that some of their fellow gang members passed the exams. It was realised that some boys in the gang like Bruce and Brian would put extra effort reading, while other gang members sat around discussing what they saw and did the previous nights in the town. At the end of the year, Brian, Bruce and some other few boys did well while the majority failed. And at the end of the 3rd year in secondary, some of the gang boys were expelled from school due to poor performance and bad behaviour. This shows that while some of the gang boys thought the rest of the school boys were waiting for them as they had their fun, they did not realise that the rest moved on with their studies when alone.

Even within the gangs, some boys thought gang activity was the same for all and did not realise that among them, some were still moving forward and leaving them behind. They just carried on doing some things as a group and lost individual focus on their education. Only few members like Brian and Bruce took an extra step to read hard and pass. Do not be deceived by peer pressure. Stay focused. Otherwise the rest of the world will move forward while you lag behind.

My very own example when my school principle sat me down in her office and gave me an eye-opening talk was when I was in boarding secondary school. It was a girls' only school and we had students from all social categories. We had the children of prominent politicians like the president, vice president and even ministers. We also had students from poorer families. I was one of those from a middle-income family. The competition to get to university was really stiff after secondary school. Everyone knew that you had to pass very highly to get a government sponsorship bursary. If you didn't get it, your parents would have to pay for university. Being from a middle-income family, I had no choice but to focus on my studies, because if I didn't pass highly, I may not afford to go to university. In my third year of studies, I became friends with the, daughter of one of the prominent and rich political families in the country. We soon became notorious for talking in class while the teacher was teaching, we paid little attention and instead sat at the back of the class and talked throughout the lesson. Sometimes we laughed so loud that we disrupted the class. She would tell me all these amazing stories from her holiday travels abroad. She even told me how after secondary school, her parents were planning to pay for her to go to university in Europe. That was something I could not even afford to dream of. Luckily for me, the school principle, or headmistress as we called her, got to know about us and she called me in her office. She reminded me of the fact that although I thought we were moving at the same pace with my friend, I was actually being left behind. This is because I was from a poor family who could not afford to pay my university if I didn't pass well enough for a university bursary. Yet I was foolishly playing around in class time with a person who had all the money to finance their education if they didn't pass well! She told me to think about my individual situation and focus on my study! That was a big lesson for me! After that talk, I was more focused because I could not imagine not getting the grades to go to university for free.

I was very lucky to learn the lesson early because I eventually passed well and made it to university on a government bursary But not many girls got that chance and by the time they realized that they were going in the wrong direction due to peer pressure, it was too late to catch up. They were truly left behind when all along they thought their friends were waiting for them.

Always watch out for peer pressure. Focus on what concerns you and follow your own purpose. Remember your individual and family values and live by them, not what the majority seem to be following. Most of all follow your heart. If t seems wrong, it probably is wrong. If not sure, always ask a trusted adult like a teacher or parent

Agogaya nigo gabutosya.

*The little water you despise (and add in the pot)
is what makes the bread meal soggy.*

*Door het kleine beetje water waar je op neerkijkt en in
de pan gooit, wordt de broodmaaltijd zompig.
(Nederlandse uitdrukking: Het zit hem in de kleine
dingen/ kleine oorzaak, groot gevolg)*

The people from Ankole love to grow and eat millet. Millet is a brown grain cereal that is similar to wheat. It is used to make millet flour that can be cooked into porridge called *obushera,* or made into a millet meal that can be eaten with stew or soup. This millet meal is called **oburo** or **akaro**.

Making millet meal is a delicate process. It also requires some energy because the millet flour is slowly mingled with boiling water to make a thick bread. This is a delicate process because the amount of water used has to be carefully added. If you put too little water the meal becomes too hard and difficult to eat. But if you put too much water it gets soggy, sticky and difficult to eat. Once the perfect consistency has been achieved, adding even a small amount of water can make the millet soggy. Soggy sticky millet is not easy to eat because it sticks on bowls or forks and hands. So, however much you despise that little water, it can spoil your whole meal. In this saying, we are being advised that the little water you despise is not insignificant. In fact, it is enough to make your millet soggy and spoil the result.

The saying is teaching the concept of being precise. Small diversions in a process can make significant differences in outcomes.

Apart from this direct meaning in relation to cooking, it also has more diverse lessons. At a point of decision making, don't ignore small considerations. They may be the make or break points in the whole process. Small lapses in judgement could lead you in a wrong direction or to a wrong conclusion.

The saying covers all sorts of dimensions. It really depends on what situation one was dealing with. Sometimes we misjudge people. We may make quick judgements without knowing full facts. The person you may despise today may turn out to be your employer in the near future; the woman you met in the supermarket offended without saying sorry, may be the one you will find tomorrow on an interview panel for your dream job. This saying was meant to show us that we should never despite anything or anyone we meet.

One of the great prophets called Jesus quoted this scripture in *Matthew:21;42 The stone which the builders despised and rejected turned out to be the cornerstone of the whole building.* Sometimes the thing you think as useless can be the one that saves the day.

Food for thought

Can you remember any time(s) when something you thought was irrelevant turned out to be actually useful?

Owahiiga enjojo tahugira aha kurekyera enyonyi.

A person who hunts elephants does not stop to throw stones at birds"

Iemand die op olifanten jaagt, stopt niet om stenen naar vogels te gooien (Nederlandse uitdrukking: Je moet je doel niet uit het oog verliezen)

This saying was also used by our parents to teach the value of focus. This can seem direct, but it also has hidden layers of meaning. It encouraged us to keep focused on what we are doing no matter how many distractions and disruptions you may have in your way.

Of all the animals, elephants were considered to be most intelligent. They have a good memory, are very big in size and can be difficult to catch in a hunt. A person who is hunting them has a big aim and goal. This person has to plan well and have a very good strategy If the person starts getting distracted and looking at simple things along the way, they may lose the trail of the elephant and may never catchup. In the case of this saying, one can be distracted by birds eating grains in the crops. They could be tempted to stop and chase them away by throwing stones at them. Chasing the birds away is good for the crops in the garden but not very helpful in the task of catching the elephant. The birds may also make sound as they fly away, and this can alert the elephant. Throwing stones at birds in this case is seen as a counterproductive distraction.

As children, we always had simple age appropriate tasks and projects that we were expected to finish within a certain time. Sometimes there were rewards at the end like extra free play time, or a movie borrowed from the video library to watch at the weekend. Even our parents' approval of our behaviour was a good reward for our hard work. If we got a little distracted or played a bit in between, it was ok as long as we eventually finished the task on time. However, if the distraction took too long and we finished the task too late or even failed to finish, we missed the reward. Our parents referred to these distractions as *"throwing stones at birds"*

The concept of throwing stones at birds became more relevant for me when I was in my final year of primary school. I needed to work extra hard as there were a lot of assignments to finish and extra reading to do. This was important so that I can pass the notorious national Primary Leaving Examinations (PLE). These end exams were the *"elephant I was hunting"* and it was a big one. My parents advised me that I could not afford to play around with my younger siblings who had no serious end of year exams. Playing with them was a distraction, the same as "throwing stones at birds". So, every time they found me playing outside, they asked if I had finished my school assignments. If I had not done so, they reminded me that I was wasting time *throwing stones at birds*. It was initially annoying but that year, I understood the real meaning of the proverb. ***"A person who hunts elephants does not stop to throw stones at birds"***

I am glad I followed the advice because in the end, I performed so well that I was actually the best performing student in my year, not only in my school but also in the whole country. Oh, at that age, the reward was so big, like the big elephant, because in addition to passing well, I received my first ever cash prize, my very own money! I was so proud of myself!

In another example, imagine a football player on the pitch playing a very important game. During the game he may be insulted by an opponent or fans from the opposing team. If he does not focus on the game, he may get hurt by the insults and even try to fight back, by insulting them in return, or fighting the opponent. If caught, he could be given a red card and he misses playing the rest of the game. He can even lose his focus and the other team scores a goal. First, he lost focus on the game, secondly, he forgot his purpose which was to score and win the match. He stopped focusing on the game and started to throw a few stones at some random birds. That could cost him and his team the game.

The big lesson is to learn to stay focused, ignore the distractions (*birds)* because they are not really that important to the goal you want to achieve. Remember they are just distractions. Keep your focus and the reward will be amazing.

Food for thought

Can you think of times when you have lost focus and started to "throw stones at birds"? I am sure there are many times when you may have been distracted from your goal. What are some of the actions or activities that you could categorise as distractions? The list is endless. It can start with: TV, Video games, playing... Please complete the list

A younger man teaching a community of elders)

CHAPTER 8:

GOODNESS/ SOCIAL BEHAVIOUR

This chapter contains a collection of a few of the sayings that taught me to be open to learning, but also seek to be with people of good character. I also learned to be a good example for my siblings and others in general.

A younger man teaching a community of elders

N'omuto nateera engoma abakuru bazina.

A young one can also play the drum for the adults to dance

Ook een jongere kan op de trommels de maat slaan waarop de volwassenen kunnen dansen

This must be a favourite one for every child. It literally means that a young child can also play the drum for the adults to dance. In the Luganda language it is *"N'omuto akubila abakulu engoma nebazina"*

This is about a young child having an opinion of their own. They could even advise an adult in some cases. It encourages adults to take them into account and listen to them too.

When we were growing up, young children were not known to advise older people. In fact, there is a saying that *"children should be seen (in action) and not heard"*. This meant that although children could have opinions, they were not expected to voice these out. Especially if these opinions were in contradiction to adults, or if the opinions were advising adults. Children could not contribute to a conversation by adults. It didn't mean that children were dumb, they were just expected to be modest and quiet because they lacked the experience in life that adults had.

This saying served as a reminder for elders that children can sometimes know enough to express their opinions. They could even advise adults in some cases. Generally, someone younger can express their opinion to or even advise someone older. A 45-year-old advising a 60-year-old person also falls in the same category. Hence sometimes the adults can dance to the drumming of children. This proverb could be used when a parent was being stubborn to the request or ideas of a child. This was to teach adults not to always dismiss children's ideas, but sometimes listen to them.

The lesson is very good in this day and age when technology and developments advance so fast. Most times, children can invest the time and effort into learning certain aspects of new technology and hence be able to advice. Children also can learn fast and adapt to the fast-changing ideas of the world today. Some good innovations and ideas are created by children. Children still have the ability to see things differently, compared to adults who may be set in their ways and unwilling to change.

There is a delicate balance. It does not mean that a child should continuously argue with the ideas and authority of the adult just for the sake of being heard. Children can be taught to voice their opinions with respect and patience. Adults can also learn to be more patient to listen to children's opinions and when possible factor them in decisions. This can be very important in making family decisions as this exposes child early to decision making skills and processes. In families where children are part of the decision-making process, there is more peace and success as all are on the same page.

<u>Food for thought</u>.

Can you think of examples of decisions in the family where children can contribute ideas?

Can you also think of scenarios where you could be able to give some advice to your parents?

Abaragaine Tibetana.

Those who have agreed on something don't need to remind each other.

*Zij die ergens afspraken over gemaakt hebben, hoeven
elkaar daar niet meer aan te herinneren
(Nederlandse uitdrukking: afspraak is afspraak)*

Okuragana means to agree on something; to come to an understanding. The Dutch say **"afspraak is afspraak"** to mean what you have agreed upon, you have to keep as agreed. *Afspraak* means agreement in Dutch.

While growing up, I knew that once elders instructed me to do something and explained it, it was a kind of agreement. I had to do it as instructed. So once parents instructed you to do something, they didn't expect to keep reminding you or showing you how to do it.

When you agree, you make **endagano**. The agreement can be any nature of agreed plan of action.

Here were some of the "endagano" – agreements I had as a child. The times are approximations and were not always exact as depicted.

About 06:30- Wake up, make my bed, get water from the well, pack my lunch, have breakfast, dress into my school uniform

About 07:30- go to school, study, learn and behave well. Do not get in trouble at school or on the way to school or back home.

About 16:30- back home from school, eat a snack

Between 17:00-18:00 –fetch water from well, help cooking dinner

Some conditions: If chores were done by 18:00, I could play before dinner.

About 19:30- we had stories by fireplace and went to bed right after.

This was very clear. So, our parents did not expect to remind us. Even when they were not at home, each one did our chores as expected. Of course, as children we could play and lose track of time but generally each one knew what to do.

Below are some simple agreements with my 10-year-old son and 7-year-old daughter. These general agreements are also like house rules.

- ❖ No watching TV or playing video games in the morning while still in pyjamas. This means wake up, wash face and brush teeth, have breakfast. When this is done, you can play or watch some TV
- ❖ On arrival from school: put off your shoes and put away your jackets; empty your snack and lunch boxes and place them in the sink, have a snack; do homework, bathe and then once all this is done, you can relax by playing outside or watching some TV before dinner.
- ❖ Right after dinner, brush teeth. If everyone is ready for bed by 20:30, we can have a bedtime story. If someone is not ready for bed by 2030, no bedtime story for that person.

Each one has their own age related tasks that they are expected to do as is shown in the two pictures in the chapter 2 under the saying of " *Tokagira .embwa okamoka*"- *One who owns a dog does not need to bark*

There is the freedom to choose the order in which you do your chores. As children grow, expected chores can change. Regular meetings can be held in the family to decide how and when the chores will change. There are many task lists available online that can guide a family to establish chores by age. It can be modified to fit the family in question. It is then agreed upon by everyone so it makes part of the "endagano" made as a family. Therefore, there is no need to debate and argue about whose task a particular chore is. And no need to keep reminding anyone of their tasks.

Another "endagano" we have is the bathroom routine at the end of the day. On specific days, the younger child has to bathe first, then the big brother bathes first on the other days. This way there is no arguments on who should bathe first. Plus, they don't need to ask an adult always who is bathing first. They just follow their schedule.

Most important, always remember that it is good social behaviour to keep your word. Always keep your promises and stick to agreed plans unless you both agree to change them. When people know that you always keep your word, they see you as a good person. They can trust you. To be a person who keeps your word, one has to be honest, and plan well ahead. That means you don't promise more than you can deliver.

This applies at work too. If it is agreed to complete an assignment by a certain date, then there is no need for reminders.

What are some of the **endagano (agreements)** that you have in your home or work, or even school? Do you find it easy to keep them?

Embuzi embi aheeri, otasibikaho eyaawe.

You should not tie your goat next to a bad goat.

Je moet je geit niet naast een slechte geit vastbinden
(Nederlandse uitdrukking: Blijf uit zijn kielwater, of je raakt in zijn zog/
Waar je mee omgaat word je mee besmet).

This saying relates to the days when goats (and other animals) were tied to a tree with a rope long enough to allow them to eat grass in a certain area, or grass would be brought to them to eat. This was so that they do not need someone to watch over them. This is a form of zero grazing.

Normally, a bad goat was a goat with bad behaviours. It tried all ways to escape and sometimes fought with other goats nearby. It was expected that if you tie your good goat near the bad one, the good goat would copy the bad manners of the bad one. In the end the good goat will also become a bad goat.

Although this was true about goats, it also had lessons on good behaviour for children. The saying was told to encourage us to avoid being with bad company. We were to avoid playing with bad friends. Bad friends were those who behaved in ways our parents didn't approve. It explained the fact that when you are close to someone with undesirable behaviour, you will likely end up copying their ill manners hence becoming like them. Over time you begin to feel that this behaviour is the normal way, so you also begin to do the same. This is like the English saying that, *"a bad company corrupts morals."*

Another similar one is that "one *bad (rotten tomato) spoils the rest.*"

1 bad fruit spoils the rest

In this picture, you can imagine that it all started with one rotten strawberry. But soon enough if it is not removed, the whole pack will be rotten.

While growing up, we interacted with different people in our lives. These included friends, peers, older and younger ones, in school or in the neighbourhood. Some of these people became close friends into our adulthood. We were always warned to be careful about the people we associated with. My father always said, "Show *me who your friends are, and I tell you who you are*". If you have friends who are thieves, chances are high you will soon be a thief too. If they are disrespectful, then you will soon become disrespectful too, if they are dodging school, then most likely you will be dodging school in the near future; if your friends are bullies, you will soon become one. Which means the people around you contribute to your character and most times it's unavoidable not to copy them.

It also works with good behaviours of course. If you have well behaved friends, you more likely to perpetuate good behaviour yourself. They say it works also with money. It is believed that one's income is the average of their 5 closest friends, the people one spends most of their productive times with. So if you want to improve a situation in your life, look out for people who have achieved it and spend some time with them. Ask for their advice. You will soon learn the ways and tricks to achieve that from them.

When I was young, I was generally considered to have good behaviour by other parents and adults. I got to understand that later because when friends wanted to leave their homes to visit or go somewhere, their parents always allowed them to leave if they told them that they were going to do something with me. Sometimes we went to the library, to play some sport, or help a friend. It is because I was the kind of child who always told the truth but also followed the rules. This gave confidence to parents that when their child was with me, they were positively influenced to behave well too. I was often given supervisory responsibilities in school. Sometimes, children who wanted to be involved in naughty behaviour avoided being with me because they knew that I would point it out or tell an adult. So in some aspects I was unpopular with some. But I didn't mind that at all.

We need friends of all kinds, young, old, small, big, tall, short, cheerful, serious etc. But when we are to choose them, good character should the biggest priority. The friends you spend a lot of time with can help you be better person, if they are good, or destroy you if they are the wrong ones. We must be extra careful when we are choosing friends. Hence the saying *"it's better to be alone than in bad company."* Sometimes you may not realise that these friends are bad for you, but the people who know you (and care about you), will know and can advise you. Although it can be hard to listen to them because you love your friends, know that they are trying to help you.

Although life is meaningless without friends, it can also be worse with bad friends. Good friends will make you happy and always lift you up, while bad friends will eventually bring agony in your life. Choose your friends well and your life will be much brighter.

Food for thought

Can you think of how your good friends have been a part of improving your life? What about when they have got you in trouble? Make a list of your 5 closest friends. Then list down the good qualities about them that you think are good for you. Then also list down the few things that may not be so positive about them that you think could be changed to make your friendship more empowering. It is ok to have a few faults because we are not perfect, but see if there are any gentle steps you can take to reduce the behaviours that are not desirable.

Akanyonyi katagyenda tikamanya ahibwezire.

A little bird that does not leave its nest does not know where the crops (food) have ripened.

Een klein vogeltje dat het nest niet verlaat, weet niet waar de oogst (het eten) rijp is

(Nederlandse uitdrukking: Het nest is goed, maar het heelal is ruimer)

A bird's food paradise is a field with ripe seeds. A farmer who grew cereal crops and sometimes fruits did not like many birds because when the seeds were ripe for harvest, the birds came and ate them. And if the birds were too many, they could eat a large enough portion of the crop to reduce the farmer's harvest. This is for things like wheat, millet, sorghum, maize etc. That is why the farmers made scarecrows to try and scare away the birds. Because these crops were seasonal, the harvest was always ripe in different parts of the region. So, birds often moved from place to place following the ripe harvest. Somehow, birds seem to communicate with each other as to where the crops are ripe. They always follow the food.

Imagine a bird that does not leave its nest or its tree, or one that does not like to migrate. It will not know where the fruit is ripe. This is the same as the bird that does not communicate with other birds. Once the food around its area is finished, it is in danger of starving to death. Therefore, birds need to leave their nest at a certain point and go out to explore where the harvest maybe better. They may never come back to the same tree again.

This saying was not only about birds. It was meant to help people to have the courage to leave their areas of comfort and go out there in the wider world to explore. This could bring them in contact with other opportunities. This encourages us not only to look for opportunities within our comfort zone, but also look outside our areas of comfort.

The saying encouraged people to take advantage of the social life beyond the comfort of their homestead. It also brought to light the fact that change is a fact of life. Sometimes the harvest is ripe somewhere else, and one has to make a move hence welcoming change. You can miss out on a lot of life opportunities if you are resistant to change.

Akaana katakaruga ahaaka kati mama n'omuteekyi murungi.

A child who doesn't leave home thinks his mother is the best cook.
Een kind dat het huis niet verlaat, denkt dat zijn moeder de beste kok is

This is absolutely true. Food is central to life. Generally, mothers were responsible for cooking meals in a home. As a child grew up, they got accustomed to mama's way of cooking. They also started to learn how to cook from their mother. As a result, the best cook they knew would be their mother. When a child was able to visit other homesteads and eat a variety of foods from other mothers, they could then compare tastes and it may turn out that they find some other people who can cook better than their mother. Therefore, this encouraged people to go out there and try other tastes. Home was seen to be the comfort zone where someone felt free and safe. Aside from food, exploring life beyond the home brought a kind of variety of ideas and practices that could be good for someone. As a child grew up, they were encouraged to learn other tastes.

This saying could also be used when one was showing a level of ignorance, a lack of knowledge, about things that could be a result of not exploring beyond their comfort zone, or from being too rigid with ideas and practices. Therefore, it was also used as a kind of advice to look at other people's points of view.

Uganda has a total of 45 different tribes. All these tribes have different cultures and foods. Sometimes, the same food is prepared in two completely different ways by different tribes. For example, there are about 10 different ways of eating cassava some of which include burying it below ground till it ferments, and then using it to make a meal. Whereas this may seem a little disgusting for someone from a different region, it is a delicacy for the tribes that make it. They go to great lengths to make it ferment. When one tries it they may actually like it.

I love many local African cuisines. I especially dream of having nicely steamed green bananas "matooke" wrapped in banana leaves and served with a meat or vegetable stew. My favourite is when you serve it with groundnuts stew cooked with dried fish. This is from Central and Western Uganda.

But I have also come to enjoy the taste of *malakwang* with sweet potatoes commonly from Northern Uganda, as well as nice layered *Chapatis* that are common in Tanzania and Kenya. And yet I wouldn't want to take a long time without eating *sushi*, one of my favourite Asian delicacies. Although I love *pilau* spiced rice from East Africa, I also quite enjoy the spicy *jollof* rice from West Africa; and I have come to enjoy the taste of couscous from Arabic cuisines. Life would not be the same without the variety of Italian pizzas and pastas. The playful Spanish way of presenting food as tappas certainly adds a variety to life's culinary experiences.

I think it is quite clear that I love the diversity of foods the different parts of the world have to offer. Unless you open your heart and mind, leave your mama's kitchen and try other tastes, you will never know the expansive world of great cooks out there and you may forever think your mother is indeed the best cook.

Always remember, a child who doesn't leave the home thinks his mother is the best cook. Go out there, explore the world. Explore the food, explore the life and live it to the fullest.

Food for thought.

What are your favourite dishes that are not originally from your own culture? What else would you like to try out? Widen your list each year if possible?

This picture demonstrates different scenarios that can happen when people do not show kindness to one another and only think of doing what benefits themselves.

Shooting yourself in the foot.

Biting the hand that feeds you.

CHAPTER 9:

KINDNESS

The sayings in this chapter taught me about being kind and helping others, but also asking for help when I needed it. These were considered values necessary for a community to thrive.

Nyakwehena akenyampira naarya

Nyakwehena passed gas for herself while eating.

Nyakwehena liet een scheet voor zichzelf tijdens het eten
(Je hebt er jezelf mee)

Nyakwehena is the term used to describe someone who does things that harm himself/ herself with intention of hurting others.

In many cultures passing air in public is unpleasant and not acceptable! In Islam, it is one of the things that *"spoils one's Wudhu (ablution before prayer)*. During meal times, it can spoil the mood completely! So, it is not a smart idea to think of punishing someone by passing gas for them. This is because it also smells for the person who has passed it. Therefore you will directly be punishing yourself.

This proverb was talking about people who may intentionally do things to harm others. It advised them to think twice because they could hurt themselves in the long run. It was believed that we are all connected in one way or another. Therefore, in harming someone else, you hurt yourself too. We can be victims of the circumstances that we have created, thus the belief that, *"Those who try to harm others end up harming themselves."*

Therefore, every time you think of being mean to someone, remember you could end up hurting yourself. It is believed that what goes around comes around. Some people call this Karma. They say that *"what you give you will receive in full measure*". Therefore, always do good to others.

When you do good to others, good things will come back to you somehow. The opposite is true. If you do things that harm others, it can eventually come back to hurt you. some people call this *Karma*

Food for thought

Can you think of things someone could do to hurt others but ends up hurting themselves too?

Do you know any moments when you have been like Nyakwehena?

Enyongeserezo tebankye.

Something given as an additional gesture is never too small.

Iets dat als extra gebaar wordt gegeven, is nooit te klein
(Nederlandse uitdrukking: Wie het kleine niet eert, is het grote niet weerd)

Enyongeserezo literally means something additional. This saying was meant to encourage a giving heart also known as *"obufura"* among the people of Western Uganda. It encourages that however small something you have; you can still share it with someone. The small gesture will be appreciated. Children grew up with a giving and sharing attitude. They were expected to be generous with anyone, whether a stranger or a friend.

This saying also originated in the times of barter trade. It was a time where money didn't exist, and people bought things by exchanging based on the value. With this attitude, while exchanging things in barter trade, both parties made it a point to add something small for the other party as an extra in addition to the real product value. This did not only create a bond/friendship between the two parties but also attracted this person to do business together again. This practice continues up to today. this additional gesture always makes a customer happy and encourages them to come back to you, making the competition based on the relationship created rather than the product one has.

In addition, this proverb encouraged people to be appreciative always when something is given however small. It discouraged people who despised simple or small things given to them by others. As a child, sometimes you can receive a gift from someone, and it seems to be less than you had expected. But with this proverb in mind, you would remember that whatever size of anything that you receive, you should be grateful and take it wholeheartedly, and thank the person for their gesture.

This proverb teaches us to have a heart that gives without expecting back, and no matter how little we have, we learn to appreciate whatever you have been given, despite the value. As long as someone gives to you with one heart, please appreciate that it is the gesture that matters. This is an act of kindness which is so vital in our community and society today.

If everyone gives, we can achieve a lot as a society. Of all the things that we can give to one another, the best is the gift of your TIME. Give it and share it whenever you can. Appreciate it when someone shares a little of their time with you. In Islam, sharing your time is one way of giving *sadaqah*. Sadaqah is an Islamic charitable tradition in which someone gives with the intention that their offering will be invested in a cause that benefits an individual or an entire community in some way. Even a few minutes of your full attention is more valuable than money or gifts.

Empisi ya owanyu ekurya nekurundana

The hyena that knows you eats you carefully while comforting you.
De hyena die je kent, eet je met zorg op terwijl hij je troost

Empisi is a runyakitra word which means a hyena. This saying basically means that a person that who knows you or is close to you treats you better than a stranger. We tend to treat people we already know with much more care than we would a stranger. There is a strong bond among friends, relatives, neighbours and acquaintances. As children growing up, this proverb reminded us to treat every person close or around us with care, since these are the people more likely to rescue you when in need. More so, it made us work more in creation of social capital (people close to you) than riches. Thus, having good people in someone's life are better than riches. This gave good reason to help even strangers as these can soon become acquaintances.

A story is told of how a man from one village loved travelling, adventuring and exploring business opportunities so far from home. During one of his trading trips, he was attacked, beaten, robbed and later abandoned in a place far away from home. He woke up in a bush by the roadside and did not know where he was. He was completely lost. It was common to be lost those days because there was no GPS available to show him his location and give him directions to get home. He found himself in a strange town. He was very tired, weary, confused and with no money. His clothes were torn, and he had bruises. He sat by the roadside not knowing what to do next. He made it to the nearby town to ask for help and directions. People passed by him rushing to their different business and workplaces. Most people mistook him for being a mad man or homeless and even feared to approach him. Those he tried to consult for directions ran away in fear of this shabby looking stranger. It was after some hours had passed that a lady whom he had helped some years ago, but he had even forgotten about her, came by, saw him and she recognised him immediately. It turns out she used to live in his village and had married and migrated to this town many years ago. But she still remembered him as a kind man who helped everyone. She came to his rescue and told the people how she knew him and where he was coming from. She got him some money and a means of transport by putting him on a truck of some traders who were driving past his village. That is how he was saved. Hence, his act of kindness to this lady at some point in the past, which he did not even remember, later saved him when he least expected it. Never get tired of helping people. That is one way of showing kindness and a way of creating *"social capital"*.

On the other hand, this saying can also highlight the fact that when you are caught in the wrong or make a mistake, someone who knows you and cares for you will correct you with care and kindness. Imagine a teacher who has to guide and discipline a child they know well; they will care more than a child of someone they don't know at all. The teacher is bound to be stricter but in a gentle way. Therefore, it is important for parents to keep in touch with the teachers, continue to check on their child's progress but also invest time in developing a good relationship with the teacher or care givers of their child.

They say it takes a village to raise a child. When we were growing up, every adult in the village had the responsibility to help in raising the children of the community. Therefore, if a grown-up saw a child doing something bad like loitering or behaving badly, using bad language or fighting, they had every right to talk to the child and correct that child. It didn't matter if they knew the child or not. But if the grown up knew the child's parents, (like an uncle or even a neighbor), they would be more certain to stop you and even order you to go home. They were free to tell your parents of your bad behaviour. They could not ignore the bad behaviour of a child they personally know. I experienced this very well because I was in a school where my own relatives and family friends were teachers. My mummy was the school principle (headmistress) and so everyone knew me wherever I played. I had no room for error and could not be seen doing anything wrong! This kept me well guided and I felt very loved and safe. But sometimes I felt like I was always being watched.

Engaro ehereza, niiyo eyakira

The hand that gives is the one that receives.
De hand die geeft, is de hand die ontvangt
(Nederlandse uitdrukking: Wie goed doet, goed ontmoet)

Just like the book of the Bible says, "*blessed is the hand that gives*". It is believed that it is more blessed to give than to receive.

While we were growing up, our parents used this proverb often to encourage us to share with our friend. Sharing came with the hope of receiving in future. The receiving did not have to be from the person you gave or at the time you gave. It could be from anyone at any time. It was a kind of belief in karma This impacted our giving spirit in the long run. Most times when a child shared with another, it was encouraged. He/she received praises in return to encourage them to share more. This was a positive reinforcement to encourage giving.

A story is told of an old woman in her late 60's who had a giving heart whenever you visited her. But unfortunately, she did not have much wealth or possessions. She didn't have much to give She would feel so bad whenever someone visited her and she did not give them something to eat. When her grandchildren visited, it was fun for them as she collected yellow bananas, sugarcanes and sometimes raw mangoes for them to eat. One day, her grandchildren paid her a surprise visit and she had nothing for them. Her raw mangoes were not available since it was not the season. Even her sugarcanes were not old enough to eat. She was filled with sadness thinking of how her grandchildren would go without anything to eat. She called all of them and gave them a calabash of water to drink. She then got her tin of salt in her hands and had this to say. *"kwobura ekyokuha owaawe, omuha akonyo anyuunyaho"* This means, that "when you have nothing in your house to give to your beloved guest, at least get for them some little salt and they lick it". This was putting in mind that at the least in every home, there had to be some salt. The grandchildren laughed it off as she gave them a pinch of salt each on their hands to lick. But this became the common expression of the level of generosity we must have. Give even the very least you can get. Hence, you do not need to be rich to be kind or to have much in order to give or to have excess in order share with someone. All you need is a desire to share and you will find a way. Remember, whenever you keep holding on to something, it denies you an opportunity to receive other things. But when you let go of what you are holding on to, by giving to someone else, you have the opportunity for other things to come to you. Hence **the hand that gives is the hand that receives**. Only when you give, can you be able to receive.

It was also common belief among the Banyankole that if a guest left your home without eating or drinking something, it was a sign of bad luck. So, the least they could do is drink some water. Therefore, the host was obliged to offer something and the guest was also obliged to accept it.

It is similar to the saying "one good turn deserves another"; and also "what goes around, comes around". Sometimes we are afraid to give because of the fear that there may not be enough left for ourselves for the next day. But it helps to remember that when you give, you open the channels to receive even more. This helps us release our attachment to things and fear of shortage. We know we shall always be provided for. The Christians have a common saying the "The Lord provides." Therefore, give freely without fear of lack.

Food for thought:

Can you think of what you have that you are not using that much, but could be more useful to another person in another circumstance? Consider giving that away. You will receive what you may have wanted all along and are able to use often.

Engaro ibiri nokunabisana

Two hands wash each other
Twee handen wassen elkaar
(Nederlandse uitdrukking: Als de ene hand de andere wast, worden ze beide schoon)

When you want to wash your hands, it is more effective to wash the two hands together. In fact, one hand washes the other hand. Imagine washing around your wrists and between your fingers and the back of your hand without using the other hand! It is very difficult to wash only one hand properly. Therefore, for effective cleaning, two hands wash each other.

This is true for hands but also true for human relations and interactions. Humans function best in co-operation with each other. It is important that people work together and help each other. People have different talents and abilities. Some people are better at certain tasks than others. Therefore, when they put these to work in helping each other, the result is a more improved and satisfactory result. It makes work processes easier for all. This saying encouraged people to ask for help and to offer help. It discourages people from thinking and acting like they are entirely self-sufficient and do not need others in their lives. Communal living was more encouraged than individualism.

It is said that no man is an island. It means that to live happily, someone needs to co-operate with others. Some people fear to ask for help or accept help because they are afraid that if they do, they will then be indebted to return the favour. There is no need to be afraid because one never knows when they will be able to help or need help. I also grew up hearing people say "You scratch my back and I scratch yours". We know how hard it can be to scratch an itch in the middle of your back. When someone helps you to scratch your back, you can return the favour by scratching theirs when they need it.

In summary, we should help others when they need to because they will help us when we need, or someone else will help us when we need. Some things are easier when done for you by another person. Help each other whenever needed.

Food for thought.

What skills, talents or gifts do you have that you can use to help others?

INDEX

GLOSSARY

Abahansi- Those at a level below or lower. Could be in age or responsibility

abaheiguru, those at a level higher or below. Could be in age or responsibility

abakuru, Older ones

Abangana, Those who hate one another

Abaragaine, people who have agreed on something

Abateeki, cooks

Ageteriine, Teeth that come together

ahaaka, at the home

Akaana, A little child

akajogano, contempt, showing a lack of respect

Akamanyiro, familiarity

Akanyonyi, a little bird

akaro, millet bread

Akati, a small stick

akonyo, a little salt

Amaani, energy or strength

amagana, hundreds or plenty

Amagara, Life or good health

amaguru, legs

Amaisho, eyes

Bakiga, People from Rukiga (Kabale) in South Western Uganda

Banyankole, people from Akole in Western Uganda

Chapatis, flat bread made with wheat and fried in light oil

ebinyansi, grass

ebyaasha, wide gaps between the teeth as in when one loses teeth

efuka, a hoe

Ekiro, a day (also night)

ekyokunda, what you love or desire

ekyokweise, what you are holding

emboga, stew or sauce

Embuzi, a goat

embwa, a dog

Emitwe, heads

Empisi, a hyena

endagano, an agreement, 74

endahi, a guinea fowl

Endimi, languages

Engaro, hands

engoma, drum(s)

Enjojo, elephant

enjoka, a snake

enkoko, a chicken

entomi, a fist

enumi, a bull/ a male cow

enyama, meat

Enyongeserezo, something given as an addition

enyonyi, a bird

ibiri, two

iguffa, a bone

jollof, a kind of fried rice from West Africa

kaakye, a little bit

Kamwe, one (little)

kyangabukama, people who accept no form of authority

malakwang, a certain type of green vegetable normally cooked and mixed with peanut butter

mapengo, gaps between teeth

matooke green bananas

Nyakazaana, a servant

Nyakwehena, someone who does something to hurt another but hurts oneself

obufura, hospitality

oburo, millet

obushaza, peas

obushera, porridge

Obwongo, brains

okuhana, to advise/punish in case of wrong doing

Okukyeera, to be so early

Okuragana, to agree as in making an agreement

omuganda, a bundle

Omugisha, luck

omukoro, something to do

Omumpi, Luganda word for a short person

omuteekyi, a cook

omuti, a tree

omuto, a young one

omuzaana, a servant

omwiina, a hole

orusaniya, a flat wide plate used to serve food to share as a group

Owamaani, someone with strenghth

owanyu, from your home area

pilau, a dish or rice cooked with spices normally served in East Africa

sushi, a japanese rice dish

Tingasiga, Someone who wants to know and be involved in everything

BOOK CLUB DISCUSSION QUESTIONS

1. What did you like about this book?
2. What saying/proverb did you like best in this book?
3. What saying/proverb did you like least in this book?
4. What other books did this remind you of?
5. Share a favorite quote from the book. Why did this quote stand out for you?
6. What other books by this author have you read? How did they compare to this book?
7. Would you read another book by this author? Why or why not?
8. What feelings/ideas did this book evoke for you?
9. What did you think of the book's length? If it's too long, what would you cut out? If too short, what would you add?
10. If you got the chance to ask the author of this book one question, what would it be?
11. What do you think of the book's title? How does it relate to the book's contents? What other title might you choose?
12. What do you think of the book's cover? How well does it convey what the book is about? If the book has been published with different covers, which one do you like best?
13. What do you think the author's purpose was in writing this book? What ideas was she trying to get across?

14. How original and unique was this book?
15. Did the examples and scenarios seem relevant to you?
16. What did you already know about this book's subject before you read this it?
17. What new things did you learn?
18. What questions do you still have?
19. What else have you read on this topic, and would you recommend these books to others?
20. Do you find some similarities between this culture and yours? What are some of the differences you can identify?

Wapwony Acoli. Let's learn acoli

ISBN-13: 978-1546295921

This book is a great way to start learning the Acoli language. It introduces the learner to common items, words and phrases that they are likely to encounter in everyday scenarios. The colourful illustrations are attractive for young readers. The aim is to stimulate parents to read to their children and use these in their day to day interactions as they learn this exciting new language. Read it and enjoy playing with and using all the words and expressions daily to help increase confidence in speaking Acoli.

Work sheets, exercises and more learning materials are available on www.mollynncares.com

Printed in the United States
By Bookmasters